WHAT

*Contrary to popular belief, money does **not** guarantee eternal peace and happiness. Author Shalonda McFarland immediately captured my attention as she effectively weaved through the lives of five families who encountered true-to-life scenarios that began with a major lottery win. The Win was written with great care to ensure the characters remained relatable. The profound messages of hope in God, forgiveness for others, trust in our fellow man, and honesty for all are at the heart of this literary work of art. Sprinkled with a dab of humor and a host of biblical truths, this book is a superb teaching tool for those seeking matter-of-fact ways to establish and build lasting relationships...with or without monetary gain.*

-Angela R. Edwards, CEO
Pearly Gates Publishing, LLC

The Win will minister to each reader, each seeing themselves being displayed in one of the characters. By the end of the story, money was no longer the focus, but of the restorative power of God. The book has an impactful beginning, very creative middle, and powerful ending. I really like how Shalonda captured multiple real lifestyles, and was very relative with their behaviors. The story line was so compelling, and it left so much more to be desired from a reader's perspective. Ms. McFarland's approach was so practical, yet thought provoking at the same time. The greatest take-aways are grace, conflict resolution, biblical financial truths, restoration, and hope.

-Nathaniel J. Brown,
Psalmist and Prophet of God

The Win is a very, very good book. It is written in third person omniscient which is better, so you can experience everyone's feelings and thoughts. It was funny and also has drama.

**Mariah McFarland,
My twelve year old daughter!**

I think it's a Winner!!

**Pastor Tabatha C. Whitten,
Remnant Fellowship Ministries Int.**

The Win is a great book with a wise story format. Not only is it about winning the lottery, but about the different directions and problems each family is having. It gives information on what to do legally and professionally if you win, which can be applied to however one may obtain any large sum of money. Not only are ways shared to stay anonymous and out of the news, financial information and biblical principles are all throughout the story line where real issues among singles and married couples are addressed. This is an intriguing read that will make you think, and a teaching tool, for it contains several gems that are learnings for life. The questions in the discussion guide at the end of the book are an added bonus.

***Pastor J'von Woods,
Family Gathering International Church***

WHAT READERS ARE SAYING ABOUT

THE WIN

Can't wait to read another of Ms. McFarland's books. Hard to keep a secret, even for church folk. Have fun!

Olivia S.

Everyone has dreams of hitting the lottery. To read about church folks winning was interesting.

Sharon G.

Enjoyed this very much. These people showed so much character and integrity. When God is in your life, there is nothing impossible.

B.D.

It was quite interesting to read the different views of the winners and the pastors. Also the legal and anonymous perspective in winning the lottery. Not only was this an enjoyable read but also made me think, *what is my position as a child of God and the lottery?*

S.L.

This book was a good read. I hope there's a sequel coming. Looking forward to other books by Shalonda McFarland.

L.B.

It was nice to read a book so humble. I love the characters and story line.

Ginah

I thought the book was amazing. It made me think about what I would or wouldn't do if God gave me a financial opportunity. This book also helped me to not only give to others but teach others how to change their behavior/mindset so that they can better manage.

Elizabeth

Very good book to read, couldn't put it down.

Kathy W.

I enjoyed reading this book. Just wish I was in the pool. I would recommend reading this book. It would help you decide what to do if you are ever so lucky.

Phyllis S.

Of the many who have won the lottery, many are not happy or are in worse financial shape than before. Lottery winners must stop, breathe, and plan, just as you would with any big decision and most importantly pray for guidance.

Denise D.

The Win

Also by Shalonda McFarland

*A Christian's Worst Witness...From Being Broke to
Being Blessed*

A Christian's Worst Witness Workbook

The Win

Shalonda McFarland

Purpose Praise Publishing, Houston, TX

The Win
by Shalonda McFarland

Purpose Praise Publishing
P.O. Box 62425
Houston, TX 77205 U.S.A.

Verses marked KJV are taken from the King James Version of the Bible, Public Domain. All other versions used by permission from Zondervan via Biblegateway.com

Cover Design by Visual Connection, Houston, TX
Author Photo by Paula Boykin, Jones Photo Creations

McFarland, Shalonda
    The Win / Shalonda McFarland

ISBN: 978-0-9885651-1-1

Ebook ISBN: 978-0-9885651-6-6

Library of Congress Control Number: 2015959387

  1.   Fiction 2. Christian Living 3. Lottery

Printed in the United States of America

Contents

Acknowledgements

All glory to my Lord God who gives me everything I need, including creativity.

I thank my husband, Doug, and children Doug Jr., Mariah, Jordan, Melanie, and Rakaya who always support me.

I also thank everyone who played a part in helping me with this project. No help was too small; Mariah McFarland, First Lady Janet Allen, Ramonique May, Daphanie Atkinson, Shannon McGautha, Gwen Handy, Linda Ross (my beloved mother), Maurice and Shirley Chance, Shawn Stephenson, Duane Stephenson, Nicondria McFarland, and Pastor Chris Welch. Thank you to Steve Drake, host of Money Matters radio talk show, for the invaluable lottery advice I hear over the airwaves. To authors Derek Murphy and Stefanie Newell, I appreciate your knowledge.

I also thank the following for your kind words in the book endorsement: Nathaniel J. Brown, Angela R. Edwards, Mariah McFarland, Pastor Tabatha C. Whitten and Pastor J'von Woods.

Chapter 1

The Win

LAURA SAT IN her usual chair at the kitchen table after putting the remote control down and tried to catch the 10 o'clock news. Exhausted but hungry, she shoveled each fork of food into her mouth as she reached into her purse and pulled out a small slip of paper. From the T.V. she heard the announcer say, "And here are your lottery numbers for tonight…1, 7, 19, 26, 35, 42." Laura's attention half divided between her food and the presentation she was working on, she barely heard the voice.

The numbers quickly vanished from the screen before she could look at the numbers on the paper. "Oh shoot," she clamored after waking out of her trance. She grabbed the remote and hit the rewind button aiming it at the T.V. mounted on the wall just above the pantry door. She played it again while she looked at the ticket. "1, 7, 19…26…35…42."

Laura's neck almost popped as she whipped her head to look up, as if she didn't think she heard what she did. The numbers vanished from the screen once more. Laura reached for the remote again and squeezed it with a death grip, her hands trembling as she pointed the device toward the screen and rewinded it a second time. When the numbers came up again, she pushed pause. She had to compare the numbers on the screen to the ones on her paper.

Even if Laura would have listened to the announcer's voice again, she wouldn't be able to hear it over the ever loud sound of her heart beating inside her chest. It was as if her heart had grown louder with each passing second while it moved up closer to her head and was pounding between her ears. "OK, OK, wait a minute," she said trying to calm herself down. Grasping the ticket tighter, Laura put down the remote and walked over to the television.

She put her finger on the first number then compared it to what was on the screen, "1, 1" then she moved her finger to the next number "7, 7". Her voice was so slow and soft, she sounded like she was giving instructions to a two-year old. "19, 19 26, 26 35, 35" her voice getting more excited but slower as she moved her finger to the last number, "42, 42!" "Jesus! Jesus! Oh, Jesus! Oooh, Jesus! Frank! Frank!" she yelled.

"What's wrong, Laura?" Frank asked as he hurried around the corner with a concerned look on his face. Laura pointed to the T.V. Her mouth was open but no sound escaped as she gave him the ticket. "What?" he asked excited but cautiously as he took the paper, while still looking at her with that *don't play with me* glare. He walked over to the still-paused flat screen.

Repeating the same steps Laura had made, Frank used his finger as a place holder while looking back and forth from the paper to the screen and back down again. He gasped and smiled after matching the last number.

"Laura, is this real!"

Unable to speak, his wife repeatedly shook her head up and down. By the frantic look on Laura's face, Frank knew this was real. There was absolutely no way she could fake such pure emotion.

"Laura! Ohhhh!" Pulling her toward him, Frank squeezed her then picked her up, lifting her in the air her feet inches off the floor, as her laughter turned into tears; tears of utter happiness. Amidst the tear-filled laughter, Laura's cell phone rang so Frank released his embrace. Dashing to the table, she looked at the phone screen, smiled, and quickly answered. "Hey Tammy! Ahhhhh!" she screamed to the voice on the other end. "Yes, Girl, yes!"

Tammy's voice was still inaudible to Frank because Laura, in her excitement, forgot to put the call on speakerphone, so Frank motioned to her.

"You talked to anybody else yet?" the now loud and clear Tammy asked.

"No, not yet. You're the first." Before her statement could clear the air, Laura's line beeped, signaling another call was trying to get through. She looked at the top of the screen and saw the name of another member of the church pool. "Alright, that's them now. Let me catch it. You coming over?"

"OK, OK. See you in a minute," Tammy responded.

"OK, bye," Laura ended as she clicked to the other line to experience the excitement all over again.

Chapter 2

The Celebration

THE DOORBELL RANG in rapid-fire succession, as if a child were playing with the button and Frank shot up from his seat to answer it. In a semi jog, he headed for the front door, excitedly bypassed the peephole and looked through the miniblinds covering the small front window, to see who it was and swung the door open.

"Hey!" he proclaimed as he grabbed Don in a congratulatory embrace. Janet screamed and ran right past him to find Laura. Frank and Don heard a bigger scream as four excited women burst into acclamation, their bodies unable to keep the excitement bottled up any longer. As Frank and Don walked over to the group already gathered in Frank's living room, all the men looked at each other and yelled, "Ohhhhhh!" After more celebratory rants, high fives and hugs, the group settled down a little so they could actually have a coherent conversation.

"When we got Laura's text message with the numbers, I didn't really look at it," Jorge said, "but

Maria did, and she came running to the bedroom all out of breath, 'Jorge, Jorge! Mira! Mira!"

"Look! Look!" Laura quickly interpreted to the group.

"I thought something was wrong but she pulled me over to the T.V. and gave me her cell phone so I could read the numbers. I didn't believe it. I thought she was trying to trick me with a recording of yesterday's news."

"Speaking of tricks," Don interjected, "let's see this ticket."

"Yes, I want to touch it," Maria said.

"I want to see it with my own eyes," Tammy chimed.

"Of course," Laura chuckled, as she left the room to go grab it.

"I can't believe it," Janet smiled, as her head shook slowly from side to side. "It's only been seven months since we started the group and we won. I really didn't think it was going to happen but it happened, and so fast. I want to quit my job now!"

Don cut in, "Oh, yes, I'm calling my boss tomorrow and saying 'Hey look here, I'm out.' I can't do another day."

"No!" Laura said loudly, reentering the room. "Ok, I didn't mean to shout but come on guys we've got to stick with the plan or people will find out." Heads nodded up and down as Laura looked around the room at each face for agreement. Laura had done plenty of research about lottery winnings and lottery pools from her brief and rather inconsistent involvement with the office lottery pool at her job. She really wasn't committed to that pool, not only because there were so many people involved, twenty-five to thirty depending on the week, but because the different types of people that were involved. Half of them gossiped about anything and anybody so they definitely wouldn't be able to stay quiet about winning money. Most of them would quit their jobs immediately so that would have been a red flag, over ten people in a single department quitting would be a dead giveaway. And some of them didn't handle issues on the job well without attitude or escalating a small problem into an even bigger one, so Laura could just imagine what they would do after winning millions of dollars. She just couldn't see herself dealing with all that drama and trying to come up with some type of consensus to satisfy everybody. There were just too many moving parts for her taste so she stopped contributing to the office pool altogether.

So when Don and Janet approached Frank and her one night after Bible study to start a weekly lottery pool, Laura was excited. She quickly wrote up a group contract that everyone had to sign. Since they all were naturally a tight knit group, getting along well with each other, she and Frank wanted their other close church friends to be a part of it as well. Don and Janet quickly agreed, which is why the church lottery pool now encompassed Jorge and Maria, Craig and Amanda, and Tammy. Well, maybe Craig and Amanda. That remained to be discussed.

Laura proudly held up the ticket for all to see then opened up the Ziploc sandwich bag she had placed it in for protection, and handed it over. Each person looked it over to their satisfaction. One compared the numbers on the ticket to the numbers on their phone, someone else had the numbers from the lotto website as a screenshot on their phone. They checked numbers and dates, and when they were all satisfied, gave the ticket back to Laura to put back up.

"We're millionaires! Ayyyeee!" Tammy screamed.

"Yes, let's do this!" Don said.

After seeing the ticket, it seemed official to everyone so the celebration now became real.

"Frank, y'all got some champagne or something? We need to make a toast." Don asked.

"No, you know they don't drink but we brought a bottle for the occasion," Jorge informed. While he was getting up to prepare, Frank also rose to get glasses.

"Wait, when are Craig and Amanda getting here?" Tammy asked.

"Right, let me call them and see where they're at," Janet reached inside her purse for her cellphone.

"No, don't call; we've got to start without them. They have something they need to deal with right now," Laura quickly came up with.

"Like what?" Tammy questioned.

"Is everything OK?" Janet added.

"Yes, well...I'll tell you about it in just a minute." Laura informed.

Jorge and Frank both came back into the living room with glasses ready for the toast. While Frank set the tray containing the half bottle of champagne and long stem glasses on the coffee table for each to grab their own, Janet asked him, "so what are you two drinking," referring to the two glasses he grabbed with clear liquid in them.

"Club soda," he responded, handing a glass to his wife.

"We just won the lottery and you two can't even celebrate with a real glass of champagne?" Jorge shook his head.

"We are celebrating, but we're doing it our way."

Laura shook her head in agreement.

"Alright," Jorge quickly gave up his urge to press further, "I'm overjoyed right now." He moved closer to his wife and put his arm around her, tenderly squeezing her. "To win this money, to have this opportunity, this is indeed a blessing from God. And to be able to share it with good people," he glanced around the room as heads nodded in agreement. "Thank you for starting this," he directed to Don and Janet, then to Frank and Laura, "Thank you for even thinking of us. We are forever grateful. Salud!" he walked inward to clink glasses with everyone.

"Salud!" Maria agreed.

"Cheers," Laura interpreted out of habit.

Frank shook his head at Jorge and smiled. Tammy and everyone else acquiesced to Jorge being Jorge and their voices all overlapped with a profound, "Salud!"

"This tastes fantastic."

"Wow, what is this?"

"Yes, this is unbelievable," Tammy said walking toward the bottle. She reached down and tilted the bottle backward impressed with the gold embossed image of a spade with a capital A in the middle.

"Armand de Brignac Champagne-Ace of Spades," Jorge informed.

"I'm impressed Jorge," Don shook his head slowly in approval, "this had to cost close to three hundred dollars. This is no joke."

"I know, I almost didn't get it, I don't usually pay anywhere near that but I wanted to get something special and when I saw the name Ace of Spades, I thought, OK gambling, lotto, it seemed very fitting."

"Let's go around the room," Don suggested, "what's one thing you want to do with your money; one fun thing, just for you?"

"A Ford Mustang 5.0, white with red stripes, standard," Frank said.

"I want to travel. Germany, Paris, London, you name it," Janet settled back into the cream couch.

20

"I don't even know yet," Tammy thought. "I've been so used to spending all my money on school loans that I haven't even had time to think of anything else…I could use a new wardrobe though."

"I want to pay off our house of course," Laura chimed in, "maybe a newer car for myself, I'm not sure really. But having two new cars in the driveway may send off some signals."

"I'm with Frank. I'm definitely getting a car, something fast. A red corvette convertible or a Camaro, because I like the body style," Don said. "What about y'all?" He directed his attention to Jorge and Maria, who hadn't said anything yet.

Jorge spoke first. "We had actually been talking about something to do with ministry."

"OK but I said for yourselves, something fun, outside of ministry," Don reminded.

"We're really not sure," Maria said, "We could use a van or SUV maybe."

"OK, OK," Don nodded in satisfaction.

"But remember guys, we've got to be patient. Remember what we discussed. We must be strategic about when and how we do this or it won't look good. People will get suspicious so we've got to be disciplined about this," Laura emphasized.

"Yeah, you're right," Frank agreed.

"True," Janet added.

Heads nodded in agreement. "Well let's review the contract so it's fresh in our memory," Tammy suggested.

"I agree, but let's wait until everyone's here. How long before Craig and Amanda get here?" Jorge asked.

Janet glanced at her watch. Her eyes widened. "It's already really late."

"We need to talk about that," Laura rubbed the palms of her hands along her pants.

"What do you mean?" Tammy asked.

Seeing Laura's forehead wrinkle but no words emerging Maria asked, "What's wrong?"

"What happened?" someone else blurted almost in unison.

"Just give her a minute," Frank silenced the group, feeling the weight of what Laura was about to reveal.

"Well, they um…how can I put this?" Laura searched for the right words.

"Just say it," Don blurted out nonchalantly.

"Well, they haven't contributed this whole month," Laura said plainly. The excitement that filled the room quickly turned into shock.

"What?"

"Oh no!"

"Are you kidding?"

"Oh my."

The comments and gasps shot through the air from everyone, as the looks of bewilderment, horror, and unbelief were fixed on their faces. Taking it all in, Laura started to speak in a low voice.

"So, I don't know. I didn't tell them anything. I haven't even been texting the numbers to them this month."

"Why did they stop?" Jorge sat his glass on the side table.

"Maybe they forgot, with everything going on," Maria gave her husband her glass too.

"What do you mean? What's going on?" Don came closer to the edge of the couch.

"They've just got a few issues they're working through," Maria didn't want to talk about someone else's problems or say something she might regret so she was as vague as possible.

"Maybe, but that's no excuse, I mean we all knew the rules," Frank stated.

"Why didn't you remind them?" Don asked Laura.

"That's not my job. I'm not going to babysit grown people," Laura shot back. She actually felt a tinge of guilt for not checking up on Craig and Amanda but she quickly pushed that away because she was busy just like everyone else. Most people assumed just because she and Frank didn't have any children, they had all the free time in the world. She was the one who kept up with everything, who would always collect everyone's money and buy the tickets each week. Everyone paid on the same day and one would not pay one week's worth while another may pay two weeks at a time, or pay it all at once. She had to keep all that straight so she made a checklist and would check off each couple when they gave her their share of the money each month. Laura was a faithful member and was at every church service so they had two opportunities each week, Sunday and Wednesday, to give her the money. She'd had to remind all of them at least once to give her all of the money due before the first of the next month. What more was she supposed to do?

"So, how do we handle this? Do we split it with them or not?" Tammy asked the obvious question.

"Wow. Well, I'd want you to do it for *me*. That's for sure. If I paid for all those months and just missed the last month, I'd be pissed," Frank said.

"But you just said they knew the rules," Jorge pointed out.

"I know but if it was me, and even though I'd be wrong about it, I'd still be mad if you all didn't do it.

I'm not saying it's right, I'm just telling you how I feel."

"Oooh wee. That's messed up," Don buried his head into his folded hands, deep in thought.

"I'm not trying to be funny but Amanda does have a nasty attitude. Maybe that's God's way of saying she doesn't deserve it," Janet shrugged her shoulders.

"Hah" Jorge blurted.

Laura tried to conceal her chuckle from Jorge's sarcastic outburst because she knew it was true. Amanda was their friend but boy could she get an attitude quick.

"You know what; maybe that's why we finally won. Maybe God was blocking it before because we were connected to her," Tammy thought out loud.

"I don't know about that," Don lifted his head to speak, "I don't know if God is in this at all. I'm sure you have just as many good people as bad people who win, attitude or not."

"Well, I was part of a lotto pool at my job but stopped. But when we all decided to do the lottery pool at church, hey, it worked out!" Tammy exclaimed.

"It's true, a lot of us have done the office lotto pools off and on," Frank added.

"Yeah but, we're all good people, we all go to church, try to do the right thing and honor God, and I don't believe in coincidences," Jorge said.

"Well, I know I've been praying over these numbers each week," Laura said.

"Really?" Frank's eyebrow shot up as he looked at his wife.

"What? It doesn't hurt to ask," she answered.

Still surprised, Frank polls the rest of the group. "Did anyone else pray?"

"Not really."

"Off and on."

"Yes. I told God what he already knew. I said Lord, somebody's got to win it so let it be us. And I promise to bless the church with it."

"Yeah, I say a quick one-liner when we get the numbers, but not all the time," another added.

The answers were random and Frank was amused. He personally hadn't prayed about them winning the lottery but didn't see a problem with it either. But for some reason he was still surprised that his wife had.

"Alright, look," Don refocuses, "We're talking about dividing ten million dollars among five families or four families. So if we leave them in that's two million per family and if we kick them out, *he punches the calculator on his phone for the answer*, it's two and a half million per family."

"I'm OK with either, I've got two million, not having five hundred thousand more isn't going to hurt me," said Tammy. "And I've got that all to myself, I don't have to split it with a spouse," she playfully gloated.

"Why don't we take a vote?" Jorge suggests.

"Maybe we should see what they have to say first, you know, why they didn't pay," Maria states.

"Good point. Laura, you should probably talk to them yourself, if we all show up, they'll know something's up," Janet suggested.

"Not necessarily," Laura contested. "We can ask them why they stopped contributing and what their intentions are going forward; you know to feel them out. That way you can see for yourselves and the decision is not just based on my opinion."

Heads nodded in agreement.

"Alright, well let's finish this up, I've got to hit it in the morning. Four a.m. comes early," Jorge sat up to the edge of the couch.

"Yes, OK, well let's wait on reading the entire agreement until we decide on Craig and Amanda. But just remember these lines…" Laura read,

Upon winning we agree not to tell anyone outside of this pool or legal representation; no relatives, friends, no parents, siblings, or children, or we forfeit our portion of the winnings.

We shall not buy anything or an accumulation of things, or give money to anyone or any entity over $20,000 in the six months after receiving our winnings.

We shall continue our normal activities, not causing any additional attention to ourselves personally, our family, or our lottery pool upon any winnings.

"That's the three most important ones right now guys. Let's call it a night," Laura ended.

Excited yet tired, it already being morning, everyone said their good-byes and got up to leave.

Chapter 3

Frustration

CRAIG WAS ON the phone with the caseworker when his secretary walked in his office and held up her hand signaling five minutes. After glancing at the mahogany clock on the wall realizing how long he'd been on the phone with the caseworker, he nodded in agreement and turned his full attention back to the voice on the phone and asked, "They say the court date is set for two weeks from now? Monday at eight a.m., are you sure?"

"That's correct."

"Last time she didn't show up and I had to drive four hours to get there, for nothing."

"I'm sorry to hear that, but that's the time."

"Lady, the child is about to graduate what does she want now? I'm trying to work. I have three other kids and all she wants to do is beg. I'm doing what I'm supposed to do but she won't even let me see him. But you won't follow up on that," Craig's voice elevated.

"Sir, your account was in arrears because you stopped paying-"

"I didn't just stop paying," Craig interrupted her slight sarcasm, "I couldn't pay. How am I supposed to pay with no job?"

"Sir, the child is still your financial responsibility."

His teeth gritted and he was glad this woman wasn't standing in front of him. How dare she!

"I know what my responsibilities are. I don't need you to tell me nothing about what I'm supposed to do for my own child. I take care of my family, but he's not my only child. I had to adjust what I do for the children that live with me. So I should be able to do the same for the one that's not living with me as well."

Craig didn't need anyone to remind him of his responsibilities as a father. He prided himself on taking care of his family, and his children; all of his children. But he didn't like to be taken advantage of either and that is exactly what his ex had been doing all these years, and was trying to do now.

"How do you expect someone to provide for his own household with no income, let alone someone else's household?"

Their savings had dwindled away quickly with the obligation of paying their mortgage, car notes, and utilities. They were able to get a few utilities reduced because the family was very careful and watched their consumption during the difficult time but the house and car notes were a set amount every month no matter what; that and the cell phone and cable bills, which Craig had already noted to cancel as soon as the contract was over. The cable bill that it; because he didn't like the fact that even if he wasn't using the cable service, they still had his money every month no matter what. He was too outdone when he was given the figure for the early cancellation fee. The cable company didn't care about his circumstances, they were quick to point out that he had signed the contract and that was that.

This woman he was talking to now didn't know the great lengths he and his wife had gone through to adjust their lifestyle, nor did she seem to care. When things get tight, you're supposed to make sacrifices and do without until times got better, which is what he and his wife were doing. Everything was scaled back. No movies, memberships, eating out. Their grocery shopping list was down to the bare minimum. His wife had even canceled her weekly hair salon appointment and had been washing and styling her own hair.

"Everyone in my family understands we can't afford any extras at all. We're strictly in survival mode. And that should be the case for all my children. That's common sense. You people know everything. You know my household income and see how much my bills are. You do the math."

Craig knew the courts didn't care. Child support was based mostly on a percentage of his salary and how many other children he had so why didn't the courts change the amount of money they were taking out of his check every pay period when he was out of work? They knew his situation of course since everything is reported automatically, even his employment status. So it would only have been fair to adjust his payments to fit the new unemployment wages he had been receiving, albeit only temporarily. That was how his account became passed due, or in arrears as she put it. And now that he was newly employed and trying to get back on his feet, his ex was taking him to court again.

He tried another approach. "Everything else in my life had to be adjusted so doesn't it make sense for child support payments to do the same?"

The only response she gave was the clicking of her fingernails on the keys of her keyboard.

"You already know I'm on a payment plan to get that back current." Craig shook his head, leaned back in his chair, and sighs. "Man, I'll be so glad when this is over. Y'all don't give the father any rights. Not every woman is doing the right thing, and she sure isn't."

"Anything else I can help you with?" she dismissed his complaint.

Crinkles appeared on his face as he noted the irony of her statement because help was the only thing she didn't give him. Excuses and sarcasm left no room for help. But how could he blame her? He was sure she had been privy to way too many conversations of men who had one excuse or another of why they were behind on their child support. And the system didn't allow for excuses, not from the father anyway. "I guess not." He ended his tirade in defeat.

"Well you have a good day, Sir."

"Yeah, OK."

Craig slammed the phone down on its base and pierced his lips, not because of the woman he just got through talking to, she was just doing her job, albeit without any customer service skills, but because he was tired of going through this same charade with the mother of his son. She did everything in her power to try and get more money from him. She was always asking for something else and now he had to take off of work from his new job to deal with this foolishness. He didn't mean to be rude to the woman on the phone but it just didn't make sense how unfair the whole system was.

He took in a number of long breaths and let each one out as slowly as he could before he left his office. It hadn't been long since he landed this new job, and he didn't want to jeopardize it; he wasn't even through with the probationary period yet. He counted his blessings though because God surely provided with this new position. He was still in management but now in a different industry and with a company that had more resources than the last. His new office was a testament to that. The furniture was all made of mahogany wood and must have been bought all together because even the stapler and tape dispenser seemed to match the wall clock perfectly. He loved the classic look of his surroundings. Just sitting at his desk gave him the feel of prestige, and his confidence couldn't help but increase. He straightened his tie as he stood, grabbed his portfolio, and walked out of his office, to his next meeting.

***

Sitting at her desk at work, eating the rest of her grilled chicken and rice lunch with a side of fruit, Laura thought about how she would start the conversation, the conversation that she dreaded, the conversation she shouldn't have been put in the position to make. Not from the group, no, she wasn't blaming them, but from the couple who didn't follow through on their commitment. *I mean that's why we have rules right? So everyone knows what's expected of them. So there's no misunderstandings, no misinterpretations. That's why I made sure to write every detail down so there would be no excuses. Everyone knows where they stand so they should just do what they said they were going to do,* Laura's mind races.

She had started her day at the office in a surreal state. Just last night her world and the world of her close-knit church members had suddenly changed. Six random numbers on a piece of paper had literally transformed their lives. Even though she should have been dead tired since none of them had gotten much sleep, she wasn't. She didn't wake up this morning hitting the snooze button a couple times before she drug herself out of bed. She woke up with excitement. Yes she sat in bed for a few minutes, but only to reckon with herself. Laura had to search the corners of her mind to make sure what she was feeling was real. She wanted to make sure she hadn't dreamed the events that occurred just hours before. Frank had already left for work so she couldn't reach over and ask him. But once she sat up and tossed her legs over the bed, she quickly recalled last night's events in vivid detail and even walked over to the safe to make sure the ticket was still where she'd left it.

This day should have been nothing but exhilaration and high hopes of what was to come. Laura had actually come to work early today. She couldn't explain why. The traffic seemed the same, although today it didn't even bother her. Even the typical slowdown as she approached the George R. Brown convention center didn't rattle her, not today. When she pulled into the parking lot, she didn't even aim for the open spots close to the door. She calmly drove to the outer edge of the lot and backed into one of the spaces and sat for a while, watching her coworkers file into the building one by one. There was a satisfaction in seeing this scene and the fact of knowing that now, she had a choice. She didn't have to come into work today. She didn't have to show up for this job or any other job, not anymore. She was grateful, grateful simply to have a choice.

It changed the way she carried herself into the office. It changed her perspective about everything; it didn't bother her as much when her coworkers didn't put things back where they were supposed to. When she had to put more paper in the copy machine because someone had used the last page but didn't replace it, it didn't upset her. The gossip she overheard didn't bother her as much, and she didn't even argue when her funding request was cut in half. At the morning meeting she noticed her posture improved and as she sat around the table she felt so assured, like a poker player knowing the exact hands of all her opponents. She could handle anything that the job would throw her way, because she knew that all of this was temporary.

Now, sitting at her desk idling while eating her lunch, Laura finally had time to think about the uncertainty of what should have been a day of utter bliss. She was tasked with getting Craig and Amanda to attend a meeting with all the other members of the lottery pool. She decided to try calling Amanda first. What would this conversation be like though? She didn't want it to take a long time; in fact the shorter it was the better. Her only goal was to get the two of them over to the house tonight, but she had to be prepared for whatever Amanda might say in rebuttal to them coming. Laura definitely needed to have a plan B if her first request was met with excuses. She also needed to be nice but firm so they could all get to the bottom of this.

She jotted down a few points that she wanted to emphasize if she had to and cleared a space on her desk so it would be easier for her to concentrate. Her office door was already closed so she took a deep breath, said a quick prayer, and picked up her cell phone. Having made up her mind on how she would start, Laura scrolled and found the name in her cell and pushed the icon to make the call.

"Hello?"

"Hey Amanda, how are you?" Laura tried to sound neutral.

"I'm fine, how are you?"

"Great." Getting straight to the point Laura continued, "I hate to call you at work but we're meeting tonight and need you and Craig to be there."

"Why?"

"Well, you guys haven't paid this whole month and we need to know what your intentions are."

After a long sigh she said, "Yeah, Craig and I discussed it and we just don't want to spend that kind of money right now so we're getting out."

Laura listened intently. Amanda's tone wasn't sarcastic or combative, but sad. Her response wasn't cold but calm and was clouded with a tinge of regret so Laura treaded lightly. "I understand, but we all agreed on how we would conduct this so there won't be any confusion. You know you're supposed to put that in writing."

"I know. There's just been a lot of things going on lately."

"I know how that can be. Well, you can explain it to us tonight. Can both of you be there?"

"Yes, I'll tell Craig," Amanda reluctantly agrees.

"Thanks. See you tonight," Laura says in a hurry before Amanda can change her mind.

"O.K. Bye," Amanda ended.

After Laura hung up, she sent a group text. *Meeting tonight confirmed. EVERYONE will be there.*

Satisfied with the outcome, Laura finishes her last piece of fruit and puts her lunch pail inside the bag under her desk. Just when she toggled her computer mouse to start back working, a thought hit her. *What if Craig doesn't agree to come and changes Amanda's mind?* That was indeed possible since Amanda hadn't asked Craig yet. She thought about sending Amanda a text message asking her to please let her know if anything changes but that would just give Amanda and Craig an out. She didn't want to do that. They really needed to be there, the stakes were too high. They also knew how much coordination it took to get everyone together so hopefully they wouldn't renege. If that ended up being the case, at least she knew they would call first; they wouldn't just not show up. And if they did try to call and back out of it, she'd have to get Frank involved.

Chapter 4

The Reveal

EVERYONE ARRIVED AT Frank and Laura's house. having to hide their excitement and giddiness and take care of the business at hand, hearing what Craig and Amanda had to say as to why they had stopped paying their weekly portion for the pool, and why they didn't say anything about it. They needed to come clean as to why they didn't follow the agreement and why they hadn't communicated their intentions in writing. All of them were friends so this meeting was a bit awkward for all. Not only did everyone have to hide their intense happiness, but they had to sit in judgement over this couple, their fellow church members and form their personal opinion and a group consensus as to what to do about the situation. They had to do this quickly and also had to be prepared to inform them that they had, despite unbelievable odds, won the lottery, but because Craig and Amanda chose not to abide by the rules, and blatantly decided not to communicate, they effectively removed themselves from the pool, thereby disqualifying them and they would not have any rights to the winnings.

The doorbell rang and everyone put their game faces on and braced themselves for the meeting. They mentally had to decide what information was important or menial to the decision they were about to make. Would their clothes look new? If so, then they could have paid their dues rather than buy new outfits. Would they look suntanned? If that was the case, more than likely, they went on a trip and didn't prioritize their commitment to the church pool.

Frank answered the door and led Craig and Amanda to the living room. They walked in wearing neatly ironed jeans, Craig donning a polo shirt, and Amanda with a red top on. Dangling from her arm was a beige Michael Kors handbag, one Laura remembered admiring at a church function earlier that year. Craig wore canvas shoes and Amanda, what looked like a pair of Clarks. Nothing was extravagant or out of the ordinary. Amanda smiled from the corner of her mouth and rubbed her hands together a couple of times. Craig said hello and greeted everyone with a raised hand. Laura broke the ice and met them with a hug, then one by one, each person acknowledged them.

Because the group had to make a decision, and they wanted to make the right one for everyone involved, their eyes of judgement pondered every detail. They took notice of Craig and Amanda's demeanor, the way they walked, and what they said and didn't say.

After the salutations, the air in the room was one of "let's get to it." Everyone's eyes looked intently on Craig and Amanda as they sat in the "hot seat" to explain their reasons for not contributing.

"Well, I guess I'll get straight to the point," Craig started. "Amanda is out of work and I just found a new job.

Laura looked at Amanda, surprised that she didn't tell her before now, nor correct her on the phone earlier when she apologized for calling her at work. "She's been looking for a job for a month now. I was out of work for four months and it was eating away at our emergency fund and it just didn't seem wise to keep spending fifty dollars a month on lottery tickets. And even though I was out of work, I still had to pay child support. I'm barely supporting my own family but I'm supposed to just find some money for someone else's household, and on top of that I think my child's mother asked for an increase so I've got to go back up there to meet the judge for that, so right now we're gonna have to get out and revisit it when Amanda finds some work."

Silence.

"Y'all are all looking at me pretty intensely. I know we should've told you beforehand that we were out of the pool but I didn't know it was that serious," he hesitantly laughed.

"Would you be willing to pay the month you missed?" Laura asked.

Amanda looked at her husband in disbelief.

"Yes," Craig said reluctantly. "That would only be right, since we didn't tell you. Amanda, will you write a check?"

"Great," Laura said. "Craig, Amanda, would you excuse us for a minute? Come." She beckoned them to the kitchen.

"What's this?" Craig laughs.

"Yeah, I'm giving you the money, what else is there to discuss?" Amanda asked, obviously annoyed.

"Just be patient please. Wait here," Laura motioned and bolted back to the living room.

She reentered the room and saw everyone's faces deep in thought. "Alright, what do you think?"

"Yes, give it to them. If I would have lost my job, I would have done the same thing," said Jorge.

"I agree," Maria rubbed her husband's back, proud of his answer.

"Yeah, it'd be different if we had only been doing this for a couple of months but it's been what, seven, nine? He's proven himself," Don added.

Janet nodded in agreement with her husband.

"Tammy?" Laura questioned.

"I'm OK with it, I mean sure technically they didn't do what they were supposed to."

"No, there's no technically, they went against the contract. They were wrong," Frank interrupted.

"True, but" Tammy continued, "even though they might not deserve it, I'd feel really bad not giving it to them."

"So is that a Yes or No?" Laura prodded.

"Yes," Tammy said definitively.

"Frank?" Laura looked at her husband.

"Do you think they'd do it for one of us?" Frank asked as he looked around.

"Good question," Don said.

"Craig probably would but Amanda, I don't know." Janet shook her head.

"She's our friend but she's something," Tammy chuckled.

"Well," Laura said, "while you're thinking about it, my answer is yes. I went through all these different scenarios in my mind., what if…and why didn't they, and I just thought about grace." She sighed. "This is an opportunity to show God's grace."

"Or his judgment," Frank smirked.

Laura cut her eyes at him.

"I'm just playing, it's a yes for me too," Frank lamented.

"Yes!" Laura exclaimed. "So we're all in agreement?" She checked around the room one more time and everyone confirmed. "Great, let me get them."

As she was going back to the kitchen, Craig and Amanda were walking out. "Hey," Laura said.

"Laura, this is really awkward. Tell everyone bye for us, we're gonna head out," Craig said.

"No, I was just coming to get you guys. Come on we have something to share with you."

"Come on Laura, we're already pretty embarrassed. We left the check on the counter." He went back to retrieve it. "Here you go," Craig handed it to her and continued walking toward the front door.

"No, you want to hear this."

"It doesn't matter. We'll see you guys later."

"Do not walk out that door!" Laura's voice rose.

Taken aback, they both look at Laura then Craig looked at Amanda.

"O.K. Laura, O.K.," Amanda threw her hands in the air.

After walking back to the living room, Laura sat next to Frank and waved for Craig and Amanda to return to their seat.

"Thank you both for your patience, I know this wasn't easy. We have some news for you," Laura began. "Well...the reason we wanted you to come over here tonight and the reason we were hounding you a bit was..."

"Because we wanted to do the right thing," Frank interrupted.

"Yes." Laura said.

"It's no problem," Craig said. "We understand. It's been nice," he looked at Amanda, "and like I said we may get back in later on, we'll have to see."

"Yeah, no, that's fine. That's not what we meant," Laura said.

"We won some money," Don cut to the chase.

"Ah man, that's great. Doggit!" Craig said, knowing they had missed out.

"Ugh, and we missed it! Wow." Amanda closed her eyes and let her head fall to the side and rest in her hand.

"If you don't mind me asking, how much?" Craig asked.

"Ten," Tammy said, deliberately being evasive.

"Whoa, that's nice. That's two thousand a piece. Well, it would have been. Man, we could have used that money too," Craig clapped his hands in disbelief. "But hey, it's all good. We thank you for telling us."

"But that's the good part," Maria said. "We all are in agreement to cut you in anyway."

"You mean," Craig clears his throat, "you're going to give it to us anyway, even though we didn't pay?"

"Yes," Janet confirmed.

Craig put his head down in disbelief and shook it slowly. He softly said, "Thank you. We sure can use it." He looked at his wife and saw her eyes welling up with tears so he put his hand on her leg.

"Yes, thank you. You guys that is so nice of you. Really, we can't thank you enough," Amanda wiped an escaped tear from her cheek.

"That's not all," Laura smiled. "Tammy said ten. You assumed it was ten thousand dollars."

Craig and Amanda redirected their gaze from Laura to everyone else in the room.

"It was diez millones!" Jorge screamed.

41

Everyone laughed as Craig surveyed their faces then looked back at Jorge. "What man?"

Jorge jumped to the edge of the seat, his smile widened, filling his face. "Diez millones!" Jorge screamed louder.

"Come on English, Jorge. I keep telling you, speak English around me, man."

"Ten million dollars!" Maria shouted the interpretation.

Craig stood straight up.

Amanda's mouth was wide open.

Craig looked at Frank. "Man, what did she just say?"

Frank laughed. "Yeah man, we won ten million dollars."

"Ahhhhhhhhhhhhhhhhhhh!" Amanda shrieked.

"Nah, y'all quit playing with me." Craig scratched his head.

"Laura!" Craig demanded as he walked over toward her grabbing her arms in excitement. "Now, I know *you're* not gonna play no tricks on me. Tell me now, come on, t-t-t-tell me," his voice began to stutter, "how much money we won."

"It's true; we won ten million dollars!" Laura grabbed his shoulders as if to shake the belief into him, as others added their assurances in their own words.

"And y'all are gonna split that with us?" Craig burst into tears as his body sank into the nearest seat. "Oh Lord, thank you!"

"Mmmmm, mmmmm!" Amanda wailed.

There wasn't a dry eye in the whole house as everyone started hugging each other and praising God.

Chapter 5

Down to Business

THE DAY ARRIVED to make sure everything was taken care of legally with the winnings. In an abundance of caution Laura set up the appointment on a Saturday when the prestigious office of Brown, Roberts, & Dean Law Group was normally closed, so the pool members wouldn't be seen by anyone else, especially other church members. She also asked them to arrive at separate times and come through separate entrances to the building. Even though the law office was closed, there were other businesses in the building and she wanted to avoid anyone noticing any of them by themselves, and especially not as a big group. That would be too obvious to be just a coincidence.

Because they spaced it out, no more than one couple at a time was in the elevator. When Laura first gave out the suggestion, she was hit with a few groans and backlashes of *"Are you serious?"* and *"Is that really necessary?"* But eventually everyone had agreed to the extra precaution.

As they each came through the front doors of the law practice, they greeted each other with hugs and bouts of revelry. Their personal lawyer was the only one there, since Laura didn't even want the secretary to see the pool in a group. She didn't want to take any chances of the secretary murmuring to another employee and spreading rumors about this. Even though most firms make their employees sign confidentiality agreements, they didn't always work. Knowing privileged information about a high profile client, especially a celebrity could result in a nice payday from one of the tabloids. That was something many employees wouldn't pass up; and it would be hard to prove the leak came from a particular person.

No one in the lottery pool were celebrities but a ten million jackpot, found out, would catapult all of them into that status, and not in a good way. If they all showed up at the same time, it would definitely be noticed. The secretary could take a wild guess as to why five different families had come into the office at the same time, to see the same lawyer. It would be easy to do. What else could it be but a winning lottery pool? She may not expect it to be a church lottery pool, but a lottery pool nonetheless. So here they were all together, with their legal advisor, ready to hear what he had to say to them about their new-found wealth and how they should handle it.

Mr. Roberts greeted them and gestured toward a conference room. He then went to lock the front doors for safety and returned to them.

"Congratulations is definitely in order!"

Thank you's, smiles, and head nods were scattered across the room.

"So how did you find me?" He directed his question to Laura, the one who made the phone contact.

"I searched the internet for law firms that concentrated on estate planning, and of the ones that popped up, I went to each of their websites. Of the names listed on their rosters, I looked at their pictures and bio and yours stood out to me, so here we are."

"Well, I'm glad you're here; I'm glad you picked me. And what was it exactly that caused you to choose me?"

"You're board certified in estate planning and your bio says you've worked with some clients that won the lottery and you have over twenty years of experience in income, estate, and gift taxes. Your write-up also said you are well versed in trusts and LLC planning."

"Yes, that's right. O.K. Well, first off, you'll need a team of people, not just me. You'll also need an investment advisor, a CPA, and a certified financial planner. They'll give you advice on how to structure your payout; whether you all want a lump sum or annual payments. I've got to tell you, in my experience, it's better to go with the annual payments because most of my clients blow it the first few years, and it's best to mess up with a portion of your money versus the whole thing. But if you take the annual payments, that also means you will be tied to each other for several years and a lot can happen in that time. A huge plus for annual payments is the reality that it's going to take you a few years to learn from your mistakes. You may not think you could possibly spend all that money in one year but I'm telling you, I've seen it happen."

Janet's eyes got bigger and Jorge and Maria glanced at each other.

"Most people who win, they raise their lifestyle to fit their new-found wealth, and some go beyond that. You buy a bigger house, then a vacation home, you buy a car for each of you, and for each of your children, and before you know it, you've spent it all. I must say, you having a trust is a huge start, so at least you'll be anonymous. You won't have your names in the press for people to start hounding you and strangers soliciting you to join their investments. I don't know how deep you all are taking this, as far as being anonymous, but I must suggest that you have some level of anonymity amongst your families as well. It does no good to go through all this trouble only to have your uncle or children tell someone. They only need to tell one wrong person and all you've worked so hard to keep secret will be on the front page news. It would be worse than if you were a professional athlete or celebrity who gets constant pressure from family and friends. And they don't even have to be malicious about telling, it could be an accident, something they let slip out during a conversation. Something that small is all it takes. Since you don't know who in your family could be the breech, it may be best not to tell anyone; but of course it's your call to make."

"What about telling our pastor?"

Mr. Roberts shook his head slowly, contemplating. "That's not a good idea either, for a couple reasons. One, he's a person too and is not immune to accidently letting it slip to his wife, or a deacon, really anybody. You just never know how these things can happen. And then the fact that it was a church lottery pool. Ministers have different opinions on the lottery. If he thinks it's a sin, how is that going to look that not just one of you were playing, but five different families, and you organized it at *his* church? Office lottery pools are one thing, but a church lottery pool is a whole different ball game. If it gets out, how would he look amongst his peers;

other pastors or churches? I don't know if he would want that kind of attention or maybe even ridicule, from outsiders, well, even insiders."

Another pause, then he continued, "Then you may have a pastor like one of my clients who also won the lottery. His pastor was fine with it, thrilled even, but he started asking my client for money left and right, giving him a guilt trip on everything. He wanted money for the building, money for his own personal home and car, but he kept asking; using the fact that he was God's anointed. He was the worst thing that happened to my client."

"Why didn't he just leave the church?" Don asked the question that was on most of their minds.

"You'd be surprised of the kind of hold most pastors have on their members. It was extremely hard for my client. He felt obligated."

Mr. Roberts paused to give time for everything he had said to sink in. Each of them looked at their spouses and some turned their gazes to the floor or any area that they could concentrate in to contemplate the potential consequences.

"Another thing, each of you needs to figure out how you'll plan your lives when you get this money."

"What do you mean?" Craig looked at Amanda.

"You need to set a budget." Mr. Roberts focused on Craig's question, then turned his attention back to the group. "I know that may sound crazy but it doesn't matter how much you have. You *will* overspend if you don't have a budget. And you need to revisit your wills, advance directives, all of that. If one or both spouses dies your share of the winnings can be distributed out to another trust for your beneficiaries. But if you have under-age children, you may need to rethink who you'd want to raise them. Your chosen guardians never have to know about the winnings either, they would be able to take care of your children with the insurance money alone. And yes, I will go over each of your policies to make sure you have the right coverages and ensure everything is in order. I'll need to set up individual appointments with each couple, and Ms. Tammie you'll obviously be by yourself, to discuss your specific situation. The sooner the better though."

Everyone started to get ready to leave when Mr. Roberts added, "Do any of you have liens or judgments against you?"

Heads nodded "no."

"Back child support?"

"Oh no," Amanda's eyes darted at Craig, "what does that mean?"

"Yes, I do," Craig turned to face him, "is that going to be a problem?"

"You two need to see me as soon as possible."

"Definitely," Craig nodded.

And with that, everyone left in waves just as they had upon arrival.

Chapter 6

Singleness

TAMMY LEFT THE mall with a couple of bags. She had always been frugal and now was the time to treat herself to a few suits and dress shoes. It had been a long time since she bought herself this much at one time but she had earned it and was always excited to add something else to her wardrobe, anything to break up the mundane scrubs that served as her daily uniform. Tammy was a hard-working single woman who worked as a registered nurse at the local hospital.

Although Tammy was grateful the hospital she worked for did not have a strict dress code that called for only a few different choices of all solid color tops and matching bottoms, she was still limited to a uniform no less. But at least they allowed the nurses to wear pretty much any type of nurse uniforms they wanted, no matter what the pattern was. Tammy was glad she grew up in the nineties because she had seen pictures in her textbook of the drab uniforms nurses much older than her had started out with. All white, and dresses at that, with thick stockings and a matching hat that you had to pin to your hair. The look made her laugh even now as she wondered if her concern for people would have kept her focused on pursuing a career in nursing, or would her love for fashion had won over. She still wasn't sure but was glad she lived in this time because nurses' uniforms had come a long way. Now Tammy could wear any print or style that was unique to her, anything from Betty Boop or Tweety Bird, to one that had a Mandarin collar. But they were still uniforms, and something that she wouldn't be seen in on any day other than a work day.

Stepping out of her favorite department store, JC Penney, one of the main stores in the mall, having its own main entrance and exit doors, she walked to the parking lot toward her car with a sense of satisfaction. Even with her new-found wealth, she wanted to continue her simple lifestyle so this purchase was still within her normal post-student-loan budget. Other single women her age would have gone to Neiman Marcus or some other premium retailer but not Tammy. You don't just spend money because you have it, was her attitude. And she never was the type to care about name brands or trying to impress anyone. If she liked it, she wore it, no matter where it came from. She frequented JC Penney because she liked their style of clothes and the reasonable prices. Also, whether she bought it in the store or online, she knew it would fit her just right, now that she had figured out the brand that fit her tall frame the best. She actually still planned on shopping at her usual thrift stores, which she did almost exclusively for a long while, but not today.

Tammy had recently paid off her student loans, before she and her church members had won the lottery. It took her four long, dedicated years of sacrifice but she finally did it. She made her last payment over the phone asking what the payoff was after the interest was prorated over the days that had passed within that month and even waited until she had received the notice in the mail where she could see in writing with her own eyes that her balance had been paid in full. Only then had she decided to treat herself because of what she'd accomplished. And she vowed to never again owe anyone else any money. She was finally living!

She breathed in the summer air and took in the sunshine that beamed from the cloudless sky. Tammy loved the Houston weather, heat and all. It felt like summer most of the year and sometimes even during Thanksgiving and Christmas. There were many unpredictable days however, when the weather decided to flip flop and satisfy non-natives with a Texas winter in the off season, even showing off all four seasons in one day, which Tammy didn't think she'd ever get used to. Waking up to forty degrees but leaving work to the high eighties was a bit much for her and everyone else, which was evidenced by the spike in patients whose bodies were caught off guard by the erratic changes. And aside from a few rainy stretches that forced their way into the almost year-long summer, she loved it.

Another plane buzzed overhead and Tammy thought about the possibility of doing something else for herself now that she wasn't working nonstop. Now that she didn't have to work all the extra overtime she actually had time to breath, time for some normalcy, and time to do things she wanted to do, not what she had to do. Her life was like clock-work now. She worked eight to five every day and was off on the weekends. This was a big switch from the hours she worked while she was paying off her loans. She worked every day she could and all the overtime she could handle back then. Spending as little money as possible relegated her meals to the value and ninety-nine cent menus of the fast food chains, which she only ran through when she didn't have enough time to fix herself something to eat between shifts and much-needed sleep.

Now she was coasting. On Wednesday nights she went to Bible study and one Saturday out of the month she volunteered wherever her heart led her. Her social network consisted primarily of her fellow church goers, and Sundays were the main social hour.

No responsibilities beyond herself, no children, and in her opinion, no highly-demanding job, Tammy was in her element and having a great time, which is why the smooth-looking man who was staring at her, caught her off guard. He almost scared her because she was way too distracted with her thoughts. How long had he been looking at her? She now realized that she hadn't really been walking but waltzing, whimsically floating around in her own daydream, which was dangerous even though in broad daylight. She quickly turned and looked on all sides of her, making sure she wasn't a target of a second or even a third person that was part of some quick robbery attempt. Always on the side of caution, Tammy started walking faster toward her car.

"Excuse me, Ma'am. Ma'am, excuse me, please!" He was nearly yelling to make sure she heard him over the cars driving in the parking lot.

Tammy made it to her vehicle and quickly turned around. "Uh, yes?" she answered as he jogged over to her.

"Huh," he lightly laughed, "I'm not gonna rob you." He noticed her clutching her purse and bags tighter. "I saw you at church Sunday but you left so fast, I didn't get a chance to say hello."

Tammy stood there alert, then finally relaxed her shoulders. "Oh yes," she chuckled, getting a closer look. "I remember you." Whoa. Did she ever, he was gorgeous! She'd never seen him up close.

"My name's Jerome."

"Hi. I'm Tammy."

"Tammy," he repeated and nodded in satisfaction. "Here's my number." He handed her a small piece of paper. "Call me. I'd really like to get to know you."

Before she could say another word, he smiled and walked away. Tammy stood there and watched him for a few steps then she turned to look over both shoulders as if she wanted to see if someone else had witnessed this. Then she was motionless for another couple of seconds wondering what in the world had just happened.

Why did she even take the piece of paper? And how could he have even written his name and number so quickly. He didn't do it in front of her. When he approached her he already had it ready. So how long had he been watching her? Or does he always keep ready-made papers with his information on it to hand out to any woman who piques his interest?

Jerome, after walking away from Tammy, entered the mall almost in a trance. What had just happened? His mind was so cloudy he couldn't think straight. His heart was pounding with excitement that it reverberated through his ears. He had taken about five steps into the mall when he abruptly stopped, almost causing the person behind him to bump into him, but Jerome was so out of it he didn't even notice. He wanted to go back outside and see

Tammy's face again. He didn't even need to see her entire face, just a glimpse of it would be alright with him.

"Tammy," he repeated her name just to hear it again. Then the thought hit him. *Why didn't I offer to hold her bags?* And the answer came just as fast. *Because she was already nervous and hesitant. She would have said no anyway.* His mind went back and forth. *You still should have offered and let her turn you down if that was what she would have done.*

Jerome was upset with himself. Upset for second guessing himself as well. *Maybe she's still out there,* he thought. *She was after all walking really slow anyway. She must have a lot on her mind. She might just be sitting in her car, thinking.* He rushed out of the doors, his eyes glared to the parking space where her car once made its temporary home. Empty. Within seconds it was full again with another occupier. Disappointed but still hopeful his head swung back and forth like a referee calling a ping pong match, desperately trying to see which path she had taken, but he could not see her vehicle in the parking lot nor on the side street that circled the mall. She was already gone. What was he thinking? Why did he leave her so quickly anyway? Was he nervous? *I hope she calls. I've got to see her again.* He stood there for a few minutes debating what he should do next. He came to the mall for a reason but his mind was too occupied to think at the moment.

He walked back toward the doors of JC Penney hoping that before he reached the men's section, he'd remember why he was there in the first place. He walked past the racks in the middle aisle that held the sports apparel; the Texans, Rockets, Astros, and even a few Dynamo shirts hung there. Past the shoes and clearance section on the left, he landed in the shirt and tie section. Jerome half-heartedly ruffled through a few styles but nothing caught his eye. He didn't even remember if that was why he was there. Was he even supposed to get something at JC Penney or had he intended to walk through to another store in the mall? He just couldn't remember. All he could think about was what did catch his eye, the tall, slender beautiful woman that he had just let leave, without any interference from him. The woman who intrigued him the moment he first saw her in church. The woman who was now out there somewhere, hopefully deciding to call him soon.

There was no use staying in the mall any longer so he decided to leave. Outside in the parking lot again, he looked around once more, hoping that maybe, just maybe, Tammy had come back because she had forgotten something at the counter, anything. He even glared at the parking spot once more, knowing full well that it was a useless glance. What are the odds that the people who had pulled in after she left, would now be gone and she miraculously regained the very same parking spot? Silly. He shook his head at his own craziness.

When Jerome got inside his car and started it, he cut the radio off and sat there for a long time, thinking. He didn't know what he wanted to do next but speed up time to the day when he was sure to see her again, Sunday. He hoped she would call him before then, but right now, since he couldn't talk to her, he wanted to talk about her. He had to call and tell someone so he called his sister Barbara.

Chapter 7

Set Up

LAURA LEFT THE attorney's office again, this time by herself. She was thankful that she had followed her first mind and retrieved her long umbrella out of the trunk of her car when she had first arrived. Taking note of the darkening sky as she had pulled into one of the few parking spots that lined the front of the building, she wondered if she should chance it. Maybe it wouldn't rain, or at least not until after she was finished and heading home.

She had laughed at herself earlier for being willing to take what seemed a high risk, since the skyline was now a darker shade of grey than the building she was about to enter. Laura never did like carrying too many things and an umbrella was definitely a useless weight if the weather cooperated with her schedule, if not it would at least be worth the investment of the awkwardness that came from holding an oversized one. She let out a soft chuckle and committed to being better safe than sorry. Lottery tickets was just about the only thing she took chances on. At least she didn't have to walk far, she reasoned, as walking from the small parking lot was a much shorter distance than walking from the adjacent parking garage. She thanked God as she glanced down at her heels, grateful she wouldn't have to take that many steps on her already-tired feet.

The first few times Laura came to see the lawyer were with the whole group conducting business like setting up a blind trust so the winnings couldn't be traced to them individually. There were too many horror stories about lottery winners being targeted with hate mail, death threats, lawsuits, and being bombarded by family (even your third removed cousin whom you've never met that lives in another country), friends, coworkers, and even acquaintances will send you on a guilt trip if you don't share your new-found winnings with them. Even the beggar at the stop light seems to know you won the lottery! So, one of the lines in the lottery pool agreement stated that all parties would agree to set up a blind trust or LLC upon them winning the lottery. This was done to protect their identities. No matter what other decisions they already made and had yet to make, that one thing was an absolute, a non-negotiable. The most important detail of their lottery pool actually winning was to remain anonymous.

But today was personal business. Laura was giving her instructions to the attorney on how to give her and Frank's tithes from their portion of the win to their church. She and her husband had discussed it at length and this was the first thing they vowed to do. Their discussion wasn't rooted in *if* they should give, but on *how* they would give. They wanted to make sure their gift couldn't be traced back to them. They didn't want anyone in the church to know, including their pastor. Of course they would tell everyone from the lottery pool but that was it.

Weighing out different options, they decided to go this route. Since the law office had another location out of state, Laura told the attorney to mail the check from the out-of-state location via FedEx, exact signature required. She wanted to mail it straight to her pastor's house but then he'd know it was probably from a church member, so she had it mailed to the church. Frank and Laura both knew no one would be at the church to receive the package during the week, well not during business hours anyway, so they deliberately requested it to be delivered during the morning hours. That way, the driver would have to put it back on his truck, and after a few attempts the pastor would have to physically go pick it up from the FedEx location. And because the package was addressed to him, no one else would be able to sign for it, he would have to pick it up by showing his driver's license.

Pastor was good at delegation and would allow his deacons or his secretary to handle many business matters, including signing for his deliveries but Laura made sure to make it a requirement that only he could sign for this. She didn't want anyone else to open up *that* mail or there would be trouble; someone would talk, no matter how good their intentions were. She just didn't trust anyone else to keep this secret that was bound to get out, just by the sheer excitement of it all, if someone else opened the package. They would let that excitement cloud their judgment and wouldn't be able to handle the discreetness such an amount of money would require. But Laura was confident her pastor would know how to handle this tremendous blessing. She just wished she could see his face when he opened up the envelope, but that was almost impossible. She would just have to be satisfied with the fact that he'd be totally overjoyed and their church would be blessed!

Now, as she was leaving, the weather reminded her that it had a schedule of its own as the rain drops shot down from the sky in rapid-fire pace. Laura stood in the lobby planning her exit, with the umbrella set to expand. Not even the raindrops, nor the dark sky could dim the sunshine flowing from her heart.

***

Janet walked into the living room of their home and found Don sitting on the edge of the couch, his body leaning over the coffee table. He didn't even look up. Perhaps he didn't hear the keys unlocking the front door but surely he could hear her hard-heel shoes hitting the tile with every step she took walking down the hall toward the kitchen. Irritation grew inside of her so she threw her keys on the counter and they met the smooth surface with a loud clanging sound. The keys satisfied the desired effect of waking him out of his trance. As he looked up Janet greeted him with a "hello" and Don returned it with a "hi" of his own. Janet noticed as she had several times before, that her husband didn't smile. He didn't frown either but still there was no emotion in his glance.

He returned his attention back to the stack of papers he had been looking at. Janet walked over to him without a word and looked at what he held in his hands and saw they were investment documents. She sat beside him, making sure to leave some space between them.

"You know if we put this in the right investments, we can live off of the interest alone and have more than enough to leave to the kids," Don explained.

"That sounds fine." In her even-keel manner she touched his hand.

"What is it? I'm trying to do something." He kept studying his papers and moved his hand away.

"I need to talk to you."

"Can it wait?" Not even looking up, Don continued to study what was in front of him.

"No, I've been needing to talk to you for a long time." Janet had tried several times over the last few weeks to have a serious conversation with Don but he kept putting her off. Something always seemed to come up when Janet wanted to talk. Today though, Janet would be persistent. She would not take another excuse or be put off for something else her husband deemed more important.

He let out a sigh of frustration and put his pen down. His reaction gave Janet further confirmation that what she had decided was long overdue.

Refusing to let go of his gaze Janet continued. "I appreciate the life we've had over the years. We have three beautiful children who are doing pretty well." She wanted to say more but the words didn't readily form in her mind. "I don't know how else to say this so I'll just say it." She hesitated. "I think we need to go our separate ways."

"What do you mean by that?"

Janet looked him in the eye and poured out, "I haven't been fulfilled in this marriage for years. You know that. I've been holding on until the kids were old enough so they wouldn't be affected but..."

"Wait a minute," he interrupted, "you want a divorce?"

"If that's what it takes." She paused as Don sinks his back in the sofa in disappointment and shock. His eyes desperately searched for an explanation. Janet was calm. "I've shared my concerns with you over and over again but nothing ever changes," Janet laments.

"We just won two million dollars and you want to leave!" Don blasts.

"Winning the lottery doesn't fix our problems. We've got the same issues we had before we won. Money doesn't change you, it just magnifies who we are, and you're doing the same things you did before we won."

"Janet, I come home every night, I bring my money home. I've been here for you and the kids."

"Yes, and I do the same thing. That's what you're supposed to do." Janet sighed, more out of exhaustion than frustration and wondered how much more she should say. What could she possibly say now that she hadn't said multiple times before? Nothing she said now would be a surprise to her husband. "Look, we've gone through this before. It's the same old thing. Nothing has changed. Now that we have a lot of money, now is probably the best time to do it, since it won't hurt either one of us financially."

Don looked at his wife with a glare of disbelief.

"You just don't get it," her voice rose. "You've always had an issue with me. I don't know what it is but I don't feel cherished. I feel like you take my love for granted. You can be harsh and cruel and I'm just tired of dealing with it."

"I've loved you the best way I know how," he said flatly.

"If you don't love me the way I need to be loved what's the point? And I'm not talking about what I want, I'm talking about the way God told you to love me. I've told you before, it's not enough to just love me the way you know how, find out how God expects you to love me and do that."

"What's the problem, really?"

She looked at him in disbelief, wandering if he was really listening to her because she had just told him. "It's not one big thing. It's a cycle of many things. I've overlooked a lot of things. I've forgiven much of the things you've done and things you should have done but didn't and I'm just tired. I'm tired of going through the same thing over and over again." She paused and thought about saying more but decided against it. What was the use? So she concluded, "You can take your half of the money and really have a great life."

With that, Janet left the room as Don sat there stunned.

Chapter 8

The Decision

FRANK ASKED HIS wife, "O.K. So how do you want to do this?" They were discussing who they wanted to give money to and how they would do it, while remaining anonymous.

"Even though we went through all those precautions to protect ourselves, we still have to be careful. The problem is magnified when we give to others. If we weren't so generous, we could just spend the money on ourselves and no one would know a thing, but the more we want to share with others, the more vulnerable we become and the nosier people will get," Frank warned.

"Well, my parents have eighty thousand dollars left on their mortgage and I want to pay it off," Laura replied.

"I know you do. How do you want to do it? You know we'll incur gift taxes if we give over twelve thousand a year. Well, actually over twenty-four if we give them twelve thousand each," Frank recounted.

"I know, I know, but I don't care. I want them to be done with it. I don't want it hanging over their heads anymore," Laura contended.

"I understand."

"There's more," Laura cleared her throat. "I found out that Daddy owes back taxes too."

"How much?" he asked half-heartedly.

Laura slipped him a piece of paper with the figure on it.

"What! How in the world does he owe that much in back taxes?"

"When he owned that small business years ago, he didn't take out any quarterly taxes and he didn't file paperwork correctly for the employees, ugh it was a mess," Laura remembered. "Then the fees and penalties and interest; they all kept mounting up. He even filed for extensions but when he couldn't pay it on time there were more penalties." Her voice trailed off. "I want to take care of all of it."

Her husband just stared at her so Laura felt she needed to give a reason.

"If I don't pay the back taxes the government can seize the house or garnish his wages or maybe even their bank accounts. Or worse, my parents might take out a loan or equity line of credit to pay the taxes off which just defeats the purpose of paying their house off, so I just would rather do it this way."

"That's fine. So how do you plan to do it without them knowing?" Frank inquired.

"Yeah, I can't tell them because they won't keep it a secret," Laura said matter-of-factly. "They'll tell my siblings, and if that happens, you might as well tell the world." She paused in contemplation. "You know I can't even give any of this to Nell or Maury even if I do it anonymously, because they'll all talk and figure out it's me, well us."

"So how are you going to do it?" Frank asked again.

"I could send my mom a letter saying she won a contest," Laura thought. "Or, I could write up a letter from the mortgage company saying they choose someone every five years and pay off their balance. No, that won't work either," Laura reasoned. "She would definitely call everyone that works there, from the cashier to the loan originator, to the president if she had to, and verify that not to be true. Anyway, the mortgage company wouldn't pay back-taxes so that won't work either. Ugghh," Laura moaned.

"Well, while you're thinking about that, there are a few charities that are near and dear to my heart that I want to give to," Frank paused. "I'm reluctant to though. Well not reluctant, that's not the word. Careful, I need to be careful how I do it. Last time I gave them I guess twenty dollars each. Well, they put me in their database somehow and I started getting letters from them every month. That's the kind of stuff I don't like. Don't keep asking. I gave you what I wanted to give you. If I want to give some more, I know where to find you."

Laura shook her head. "I remember. We've still got a stack of address labels they sent, as a thank-you-in-advance gift."

"As a matter of fact, I started getting all kinds of solicitations from organizations I've never even heard of," Frank recalled.

Laura looked up. "The other organizations are affiliated with them somehow so when they added you in the database it went to the others as well." She tilted her head in realization, "Or they very well could have sold your information."

Frank whipped his head around to Laura, eyebrows raised.

"Yes. Some charities sell their donors' contact information to raise money," Laura chuckled at

Frank's innocence. "You have to read the charities' privacy statement to see what they do with your information. There is an organization, I'll show you the website later, that works with a bunch of charities, where you set up a fund and you can give the money anonymously."

"Wait a minute. People are kind enough to give their hard-earned money to a charity. Then that charity just gives another company their personal information? That's a slap in the face." Frank sat silently for a few moments. "Well, that explains a lot. I wonder if that's the reason we get all these marketing calls, when we've been on the do-not-call-registry for years. Who would have thought it'd be this hard to give money away."

Concern grew in Laura's eyes. "Frank, you've told me about the charities, and that's really nice but what about…"

Frank emphatically shook his head "No" because he already knew where Laura was headed. Treading lightly on this touchy subject, Laura asked, "Will you at least pray about it?"

Frank didn't respond but Laura had made her point; the seed was planted. She just wanted him to consider giving some money to the only family he has left, his mother.

Frank's parents never married. He was the only child, as far as he knew, that either of them had. His father was now dead and he had never met him, all because of his mother. She had never told his father that he had a son because she didn't discover she was pregnant until after their romantic relationship was over. She didn't want to be tied to Frank's dad at all, so she never told Frank's father about his son. By the time Frank found out who his father was, he was already dead. It took a long time for him to forgive his mother and he doesn't want anything to do with her so he had no plans to share any of his winnings with her.

His mom does have a sister but Frank really doesn't go around his aunt because she knew who Frank's dad was but never said anything. When he had confronted her about never telling him, she said it wasn't her place to reveal that. Frank didn't accept that excuse.

Frank was mad at his mom because he felt his father had a right to know that he had a child and *he* had a right to know who his father was. There were a lot of things growing up that he had to learn on his own; things that a father would have taught him. As far as Frank was concerned, his mother was selfish and he didn't want anything to do with her.

Laura never tried to persuade Frank to rekindle a friendship with his mother but over the years, she did plead with Frank to have some sort of relationship with his only living parent. Laura just wanted Frank to call or visit his mom ever so often, just to make sure she was alright. Laura would refer Frank to the scripture about honoring your father and mother but Frank's just not there yet.

The two sat in silence for a few minutes, both deep in thought. Knowing she couldn't persuade Frank into doing anything, she just sat quietly. Besides, she didn't know what it was like to go through what he went through, growing up not knowing who your father is, so she couldn't tell him how he was supposed to feel. Both of her parents were alive, together, and still happily married and that's all she's ever known.

She soon directed her thoughts to her own situation. How could she bless her parents without them knowing she did it? Her mind was tinkering with all the possible scenarios that she could come up with that made any kind of sense. Her dad would be no problem at all. He wouldn't care where the money came from. He would just accept it with thankfulness and that would be the end of it. Her mother, on the other hand, was a totally different story. She would also thankfully accept it, sure, but she'd want to know everything associated with the gift; from who, to what, when, where, how, and why and Laura did not want to deal with all of that. It was going to be bad enough just having to pretend like she didn't know what was going on.

"Alright, I've got it," Laura stated. "I'll have the attorney type up a letter similar to what he sent the pastor and I'll pretend to be an anonymous donor who found her name in a database and just wants to bless her." She paused again to think through any ramifications or holes in logic. She knew her plan was kind of weak but she was done for the night. "Well that's gonna have to do for now. I can't think of another way to do it," Laura disappointedly said. "And, since I can't give anything to my own sister and brother without them putting two and two together, I'll just set up college funds for my nieces and nephews."

"That's a shame, you feel it's too much trouble to give to your own family," Frank sarcastically said.

Laura gave her husband that wife look.

"Why don't you just send them both anonymous checks?"

"That's too obvious. Then they'd know it has to be someone close, that knows all three of them. I mean, who's going to give money to two siblings and their parents? Then I'd have to play like I received a check too." She shook her head in objection.

"What if you just put some money where they could find it? You know, a place they go to all the time, and they can just stumble on it?"

"Both of them? They'd think that was too much of a coincidence. Laura sighed. "Look, I'd love to give them something, they are my own flesh and blood, but I just don't want to risk it. I'll just stick with the college funds."

"Haha," Frank laughed. "I don't blame you, you know they're not gonna act right. It's a shame but that's your family. Do it how you want to, just keep me out of it."

Chapter 9

First

TAMMY OPENED THE door after hearing the doorbell
ring and looking through the peephole to verify it was
him, Jerome. Both of them were slightly nervous in
anticipation of seeing each other again, only this time
it would be more than just a fleeting moment. Tammy
called Jerome the day after he had given her his
number in the parking lot and they had talked for a
while but Jerome wanted to talk in person. It was
difficult to get the full depth of a conversation over
the phone when you barely knew the person. He
wanted to see her eyes, and facial expressions at they
talked. He couldn't truly understand what she was
feeling on the phone, at least not until he got to know
her better and tonight they would spend as much time
together as they could. Jerome was taken aback by her
beauty once more. He didn't even speak for a
moment because the natural light of the moon shown
just right. Her golden brown skin soaked in its rays
and burst forth her rich hue into the darkness. Her
simple yet elegant green blouse shimmered as the
sprinkles of light made her dark brown eyes dance.

He could not speak, not even smile. All he could do was look at her.

Tammy looked down for a moment, under the weight of his intense fixation on her. She couldn't help but blush as it was apparent that he was extremely attracted to her. She raised her head slowly to summon up the words, "Would you like to come in?"

Chuckling at his own reaction to her beauty, he managed a reply and stepped into the doorway.

"I just have to get a sweater and I'll be ready to go. Make yourself at home."

He heard her but he couldn't move. After she walked away, he let out an intentional deep breath to pull his thoughts together so he could remember where in the world he had planned on taking her to eat that night. He made sure to take a quick glance around the apartment so he would have something in his memory to complement her about later, something other than how she looked. From the entrance, he could see the dining area to the right and the kitchen counter overlooking it. She didn't have any barstools under the counter, even if it looked like it could only fit two, so he figured she didn't entertain much. A small hallway ran through the middle of the apartment and on the left side was the living room.

A door ended the hallway but the rest of the apartment was beyond it, around the corner. The walls of the apartment were off-white with color coming from the far left wall of the living room and the backsplash in the kitchen. Even the furniture was in soft hues, contemporary, and the only dynamic colors came from the accents of pillows and a few figurines on the dining table and small table that sat in the corner between the two couches that shaped in an "L" against the walls, giving the impression that the space was bigger than it actually was. Her place was nice and the perfect size for a single person.

After returning from around the corner with a dark sweater folded on her arm and purse on her shoulder she stood in front of him. "I'm ready now."

"O.K. my lady," he mustered as he walked to the front door, opened it, and motioned for her to walk through like he was a valet.

After Jerome closed the door Tammy smiled and shook her head because she still had to lock it.

Walking her to his car, parked by the curb, he opened the passenger door, slightly bowed his head when she thanked him and waited patiently to make sure she was settled in before he closed it, then walked to the other side.

As Jerome walked in front of the car, she watched his every move. Tammy wondered if this chivalry was out of convenience and coincidence since they were already on her side of the door when they walked toward the car, or if she could expect this type of treatment every time.

"So tell me more about yourself." Jerome was eager to know everything about this beautiful woman sitting beside him. Tammy gave him a side grin and began.

They talked the entire thirty minute ride to the restaurant like they were old friends. Finding out that they really had nothing in common as far as background, she graduating from a four-year university and he opting to go to a trade school, yet they both were fascinated about how different they were. What they did know was that they both wanted to please God and live right. They both had been attending church solo for a while now and were in no hurry to be in a relationship. They were both focused on learning more about God's word and were content with where they were in life, including their single status.

Jerome pulled into the parking spot and wasted no time getting out of the car. Tammy, on instinct, opened her door before she could think about it. She immediately wished she hadn't because she had forgotten that he might have wanted to do it for her but she was now so excited and relaxed she didn't feel like it was a date, but getting together with one of her guy friends from college.

She studied his face to see if there was any disappointment in his demeanor and to her delight there was none. He offered his hand and lifted her out of her seat and after closing the door, gently placed his hand on the back of her upper arm guiding her toward the front entrance.

After briefly waiting for a table to be ready, one of the greeters ushered them near the back of the restaurant to a booth, by. Jerome waited for Tammy to be seated, then sat across from her. Tammy had never been to this restaurant and admired the décor of the place. The walls were covered in cedar wood panels that ran vertically and extended throughout the booths. The tables were of the same color, and if she didn't see the crack between the table and the wall, you'd think it was all one piece. She could see in other areas where brown and beige bricked trimming cascaded down from the ceiling making arches that formed columns reaching the floor. Long stemmed leaves from some type of plant grew out of big rectangular pots that sat on top of booth ledges seemed to separate different sections of the restaurant. And the backs of the booths seemed to be taller than normal, which gave them more privacy.

The atmosphere was cozy. Not too loud where you had to raise your voice to be heard but not too quiet where you were concerned that others could hear your private conversation. Taking in the aroma of fresh bread coming from the kitchen and the entrée's around her, Tammy realized that she was a bit hungry so she grabbed the menu, as did Jerome while their waiter, introducing himself as Miguel, now greeted them and offered to get them started with some drinks.

"May I suggest three of our specialties?" Really a rhetorical question because he didn't wait for a reply. He just turned the page in Tammy's menu and pointed to a section at the top. When Tammy saw they were alcoholic beverages she wanted to object but he was already starting on what seemed like a memorized spiel. If he hadn't looked like someone who was working his way through college, she would have stopped him but figuring that he probably needed the practice anyway, she let him talk. She stole a quick glance at Jerome whose smile also offered pity on the guy. Looking at the menu as he spoke of a Mango Mojito, a Maui Margarita, and what he said was his favorite, Long Island Iced Tea, which Tammy noted contained vodka, gin, and rum, she patiently waited until he was finished. But she didn't want to be the first to speak, she wanted to see how Jerome would respond. So she just looked at him.

Taking the hint, Jerome broke the silence. "I'll just have a lemonade. And what would you like?"

"A regular iced tea with lemon."

With that, he thanked them and vowed to be back with their drinks and take their dinner orders. Jerome and Tammy both wondered the same thing about each other. *Did they drink?* Hard liquor was definitely not acceptable on a first date but Jerome didn't like it at all. Tammy didn't either, but for reasons deeper than what she was ready to discuss.

Looking over the menu Tammy was delighted to see her favorite fish and ordered the blackened salmon while Jerome settled on grilled tilapia. She stole a glance at his sculptured arms and broad chest as Jerome recited their orders to the server, and wondered if his diet was a deliberate part of a full-body regimen. As Jerome was deciding on his sides, Tammy took advantage of the spotlight shining from above them that highlighted his prominent features of a defined jaw and coal black hair that looked freshly edged up. The light also shown on his ring finger where she checked to see if there was any indication of a missing band, something she learned to do after overhearing stories from her coworkers about wolves they had come across.

"If you don't mind me asking, when was the last relationship you were in?" Tammy started the conversation.

"Over a year ago, and you?"

Tammy actually had to think about that. She knew it had been a while but it wasn't because others hadn't tried to get her attention, it was that she was on a mission, paying off her loans was her number one priority. She had been so focused on working all the overtime she could that she didn't have time for anything or anyone extra in her life. Now that she had accomplished her financial goal however, she was O.K. about seeing someone, although she hadn't been looking, nor was she seeking to be in any type of relationship. She was happy with her current situation but there was no denying her attraction to the good-looking man sitting in front of her, and the chemistry they both knew was obvious between them.

"I think it's been a couple of years."

He gave a surprised but pleased look of approval because her answer meant to him that she wasn't trying to get over someone else and that the slate was clean for both of them to pursue one another.

"What happened?" Tammy asked.

"It just wasn't what I was looking for," he glared at her, making himself clear that she was actually what he was looking for.

Tammy's cheeks turned red at the intensity in his eyes and leaned back in her seat.

"And you?"

"Same here," she managed.

"So can we sit by each other at church Sunday?" Jerome wasted no time.

She hesitated because what she admired about him was, she never saw another woman accompany him at church. That was a plus. And of course she hadn't brought anyone either. One thing she never wanted to be was someone's rebound girl. And she definitely didn't want to be talked about at church. She didn't want her name associated with any mess. She wondered if it was too soon to let people see them together at church, just in case things didn't work out. She didn't want anyone talking about her and making up stories and she didn't want to cause any friction at all if things between them went sour. What if they both started dating other people and brought them to church? That would be too much drama. She was hopeful he would be able to take it, because she sure was. Seeing him with someone else if they didn't make it as a couple was fine with her. When she was done with a relationship she didn't look back. Her take on it was that God was preparing her for someone greater but she was content to learn whatever she could from any relationship along the way. She proceeded with caution as she thought of how to answer his question.

"That would be nice," she smiled, "but let's wait a couple of weeks just to make sure that's what we really want to do."

Jerome nodded in agreement.

During dinner they had a pleasant conversation, one of more discovery. Tammy talked about growing up in a household shattered by divorce before she was a teenager and being the only child. Although she was never lonely, having many cousins that she saw often, she wondered what it would be like to have a sister or brother. She still saw her father and they talked often but like most children from broken homes, she will always want her parents to get back together. She talks to her mom almost daily and absolutely adores her.

Jerome seemed more interested in her, but he did tell Tammy about his parents who were still very much in love, being happily married years before Jerome was even thought about, and his sister Barbara, whom he talked to often. They were very close and he couldn't imagine life without her.

Dinner was over it seemed before it had really started, and Miguel asked if they wanted dessert. Jerome looked at Tammy, "how about the strawberry cheesecake?"

"I'm pretty full already."

"We can split it," Jerome offered.

"O.K." she acquiesced.

They ate their last dish almost in silence as they both realized the night would be over soon and they'd have to depart each other's company and be regulated to phone conversations until the next time they could see each other. As the evening meal finally came to a close, Miguel mentioned that he would soon return with their check and to Jerome's surprise, Tammy quickly inserted, "Separate checks please."

Jerome, without hesitation, said, "No, I've got it."

"I appreciate it really, but I like to pay for my own meal."

"Tammy, I asked you to dinner and I'm taking care of everything, really."

"I know. It's just something I need to do."

Miquel stood in the crossroads, unsure of what to do, and scared to say anything. Jerome looked at him and Miquel scurried away.

"Why?"

"Until we get to know each other a little better, I just feel more comfortable doing it this way."

After seeing the puzzled look on his face, she added, "It's just one of my rules, that's all."

"Did I miss something? Or give you the wrong impression about anything?" Jerome stammered.

"No, absolutely not. It's not you at all. It's just something I have to do for myself."

Disappointed, Jerome leaned back in his seat wondering if he should insist or give into her, what did she call it, *her rule*.

Miquel returned with two checks and placed them beside each of his customers. Tammy quickly takes care of hers while Jerome watches and deciding not to protest, he takes care of his and gave the waiter an embarrassed head nod of thanks.

Jerome wondered what this was all about and his excitement waned a little. He didn't want to make a big deal about it but he was clearly disappointed and confused. *Does she not trust me to pay for her meal? What kind of guys has she been going out with that resulted in her making this so-called rule?* Or maybe he was reading too much into this.

He dismissed his concerned thoughts for now because her smile brought him back into focus. They had a wonderful evening and he didn't want this small thing to overshadow that so they talked a bit more before it was time for him to take her back home.

Arriving back at Tammy's place, Jerome took no time getting out of the car and walking around to open the door for his date. After again telling Jerome how much she enjoyed the evening, and he answering in agreement, Tammie started walking toward her front door, with Jerome by her side. With each step her mind raced. *Will he try to kiss me?* She wanted to but didn't think she should, not on the first date. She swallowed hard.

When she put her key in the door, she turned to say her final goodbye but Jerome wasn't there. He had stopped halfway up the path and watched from a distance. Tammy was surprised but sort of grateful to avoid the awkward silence that came at the end of first dates; that nervous moment when you're not sure if you should hug, kiss, or just say good bye. Well, his not walking her all the way up to the door definitely eliminated that but she knew deep down inside, she was a tad bit disappointed.

Chapter 10

Father Figure

CRAIG PICKED UP the phone to call his son Joshua. He and Joshua have a strained relationship at best. Ever since Josh's mom Gloria broke up with Craig when Josh was a baby, she's been using Josh as a way to get back at Craig. For what, he didn't know.

Craig never did anything to hurt her, and she was the one that left, but all throughout Josh's life, Gloria has used him as a pawn to hurt Craig. She moved to another city four hours away so it would be harder for Craig to see his son. She constantly lies on Craig to Josh and tears down his credibility. Craig questions whether Gloria even loves Josh because all of her actions indicate that she doesn't. Craig feels she just wants the child support but doesn't care about their child.

But the child support is soon coming to an end because Josh is about to graduate from high school which is why the court letter and phone call with the case worker was rather heated. It didn't make sense to him why his ex would be asking for any type of modification when it would all be over soon.

After he and Amanda received their portion of the winnings, that was the first debt he paid. He paid off all the back child support, including the interest, and was now rid of that heavy burden. Now that he was caught up, the rest of the payments would resume until Josh turned 18. With the child support payments almost over and Josh about to be an adult, Craig can now deal with his son on his own terms.

The ringing stopped. "Hi, Dad."

"Hi son, how are you?"

"I'm fine. I'm about to get ready for work."

"Well, I want you to reconsider."

"Dad, I can't afford it but I did go down to the community college like you asked and I filled out some paperwork. I've got to save up enough money first. And…I don't know…Mamma's not helping me. She said she can't afford it."

"What did she do with all that child support I've been paying?"

"Dad, I don't know."

"She didn't give you *anything* toward it?"

Josh let out a sigh. "No, Dad."

"Well how much money do *you* have saved up?"

Silence.

"Josh, do you hear me?"

"I don't have any money saved."

Craig shook his head.

"I'll pay for it, if you'll just go and get good grades, A's and B's."

"How can you afford that when Mamma said you couldn't even pay the child support on time?" Josh shot back.

Craig gripped his bottom lip with his teeth. "That was because I was out of work for a while so I got behind. But I paid all of that back. Son, I want you to have a better chance than I did. This part-time job that you have is not gonna be enough. I didn't go to college and it's hard out here. It's by the grace of God that I have the kind of job I do. You need to get a degree, something, even if it's an Associate Degree."

"They say I can go full time after I graduate."

"That's great, but you need to do something with your life."

"What, this isn't good enough for you?"

Craig knew then, that he'd have to choose his words carefully. His son was already on edge, ready for a confrontation, just like his mom.

"No, that's not what I meant. It's a great start but you can do better. Don't just settle for that. You're smart Josh."

"I can move up in this company, become manager."

"Yes, you can but then what? You're not going to be able to advance fast without some sort of degree."

"What if I don't want to go to college?"

"Even if it's a trade school, you need to do something. Figure out what you really love to do and see what it takes to get into that field. Do your research. If you're serious, whether it's college or a trade, I'll pay for it."

"Really, Dad?" Craig could hear a smile come upon his son's face.

"Just let me know. And Josh…"

"Yes, Dad?"

"I love you, man."

"O.K. I love you too."

After they hung up, Craig was hopeful. He wanted so much for his son, and wanted Josh to make the right choices in life. He didn't know what kind of mindset Josh had so he didn't tell him his real intentions up front. Craig wanted to make sure Josh knew the value of a good education and wasn't going to waste his money if Josh wasn't going to do what he needed to do and take his education seriously. Craig hoped Josh would choose a college over getting a trade, so Josh can get a taste of what college is like. What Josh didn't know was that if he makes good grades that whole semester at the community college, Craig was going to pay for him to go to a major university of his choice and stay on campus so he would experience the college life that Craig never did.

As long as Josh makes the grades and stays out of trouble, Craig would pay for as long as his son wanted to go. Master's, PhD? Craig just wants the best for his son. He is just torn because he wants his son to go to college out of state so he can experience a different world, but he also hopes Josh will choose a college close to where Craig lives like the University of Houston or Texas Southern University, so he can see him more and make up for lost time.

Chapter 11

Respect

JEROME COULDN'T TAKE it any longer, he had to call Tammy to try and get her to tell him what the problem was. They had gone on a few dates and they were all amazing but at the end of every one, she would not let him pay the bill. She insisted on paying for her own meals and it was driving him crazy. Not only was he not used to a woman he dated offering to pay for her own meal, he felt it was his responsibility anyway. Tammy obviously felt otherwise and he needed to know why.

To him, it was an insult. He let it slide the first couple of times because of her persistence, but no more. He had had enough. He was raised to believe that the man was supposed to provide for the woman he was interested in. He believed in chivalry, which evidently is a lost art nowadays. He tried to take into consideration that Tammy was younger than he was, and maybe the generation gap was too big, even though they were only seven years apart. But maybe that many years was enough in this fast-paced society to change belief systems. He was grateful for the accomplishments of each generation, such as technology, and the strides made in many areas that make lives easier, but some things needed to stay the same. Actually some practices needed to go back in time, and men behaving as men was one of them.

He was old fashioned he guessed but he still thought it improper for a woman to give a man her phone number. If a woman was to pursue him it would turn him off. A man was supposed to pursue the woman and ultimately find the woman God had created just for him, his soulmate. He felt like that's what God had done in giving him Tammy but some of her ways didn't set right with him and he didn't want to go so fast as to gloss over them because they could be signs of bigger issues later. Whether they were deal breakers or not, he didn't know yet.

Jerome wasn't sure if he was ignoring warning signs that God was showing him or if he was making a big deal out of nothing; making a mountain out of a molehill is what the older generation would say. Right now he was going to set something straight with Tammy, whether she liked it or not.

He picked up his phone to call her. He pushed her picture, she being in his favorites, and listened as her number rang, but then quickly hung up. He had to gather his thoughts and pray, so he would approach her in the right way. After he prayed and remained silent for a few minutes, he picked up the phone again. She picked up on the third ring.

"Hi," her voice was soft.

"What are you up to?"

"Just doing a few things around the apartment."

"O.K. Do you have a few minutes? I need to talk to you about something."

"Yes. Is something wrong?"

"Well, actually yes. You know how we told each other that if we ever had an issue, or a problem, we'd come to each other and be straight about it; just say it, no sugar-coating?"

"Yes." Tammy started wondering what issue he might have.

"I really enjoy every minute I spend with you and when we go out we have so much fun but at the end of each dinner, you insist on paying for your meal and I can't stand it—"

"But—"

"I already know. You've told me, 'it's something you have to do,' but when you do that it undermines my manhood. And it makes me feel like you don't trust me."

It was true, she didn't trust him back then, on their first date. She had been in that position before with other men who felt because they paid for a woman's meal, they should expect something in return. So to avoid that, she started paying for her own. After their second date, she could see how uncomfortable Jerome was about it and after spending a lot of time talking on the phone with him she thought about letting him pay the next time but then she thought about how much money she had. Wasn't it unfair for a millionaire to let someone buy their dinner? The cost of going out all the time can add up quickly so she didn't want to put that burden on him when she could easily pay for it. He had refused to let her pay for anything for him but he couldn't stop her from paying for herself.

"I don't see what the problem is, if I want to pay for my own meal. Isn't that a good thing? I'm used to—"

"It doesn't matter what you're used to. I'm telling you how it should be. We've spent too much time together for you to be stuck on this Ms. Independent theme."

He heard her sigh.

"Look, that may have come out wrong but I'm trying to take this to another level and if you can't trust me to buy your meal, it will be hard for you to trust me for anything else."

"So, what are you saying?"

"From now on, I don't want you to jump in and pay for your meal. I want you to let me handle it. Let me take care of you the way I'm supposed to."

Tammy sighed again. "Fine. You can pay next time."

"Tammy, I'm not just talking about next time. Every time we go out, I'm paying."

"And what if I don't feel comfortable doing that?"

"Then we don't go out."

"Whoa." Tammy couldn't believe what she was hearing. "So you're giving me an ultimatum?"

"Whatever you want to call it, I'm just letting you know up front that I can't do this anymore. It goes against—"

"You know, I've got to think about this."

"What is there to think about? Ask any man and they'll tell you the same thing."

"I will."

"But don't ask these youngsters, especially the ones with their pants hanging down. They're not being taught anything. All they want is what they can get."

"What does that have to do with anything?"

"If you were to go out with someone like that, not only would you pay for your own meal, they'd ask you to pay for *them*. They're not gonna respect you. How can they respect you when they don't even respect themselves? So if you ask a man, ask a man who respects himself enough to cover his behind."

Tammy's chuckle slipped out. "Fine."

"So what time do you want me to pick you up tomorrow night?"

"I'm not sure about it now," Tammy didn't know if he was trying to be controlling or what. He did just give her an ultimatum. She basically had no say in the matter. She got how he felt. Well, she understood his explanation, but she didn't agree. So was that the way it would be if they were married? Anytime she disagreed with something he would take her choices away by putting his foot down? Maybe it would have been different if they were officially a couple; with him actually asking her to be his girlfriend, but he hadn't done that. So why did he think he had the right to take her choice away? "We'll see."

"Tammy, don't do this," he couldn't believe she was reacting this way over something so simple. She was acting like a spoiled princess who wasn't getting her way. Is that the way she would respond if they were married? He explained why he didn't like her paying for her own meal but she didn't accept his reasoning. There are bound to be many disagreements between a husband and wife and sometimes the wife might not fully understand why her husband took a different route on an issue. She'd just have to trust that he has her best interest and follow his lead. Would he always be fighting a battle to be the leader of their home? This made him think. All he could say then was, "I'd better let you go. Let me know what you decide."

"O.K."

"O.K." And without either of them saying goodbye, Jerome hung up.

Chapter 12

Pastor

PASTOR DAVID SAT in his oversized chair across from the T.V. in the living room, after a long day of running errands. Feeling kind of tired, he leaned his head back for a moment. His day started early, as it always did on Saturday mornings. Getting up at four a.m., he heads to his study and puts on some worship music. He always loses himself in the awe of who God is with each passing song. He allows Him to speak to his heart as he reads his Bible and prays. After a couple of hours, he'll head to the kitchen and get himself something quick to eat, trying to be as quiet as possible so he won't wake his wife Loretta. Then he heads to church to finish his sermon notes that he'd prepared throughout the week and spend more time with God in prayer. After that, he picks up his dry cleaning, goes to the post office, and heads out to lunch with his fellow pastor friends for conversation and encouragement.

Now that he was home, all he wanted to do was rest and watch a little T.V. or as his wife would say, let the T.V. watch him, because it wouldn't be long before she would hear the sounds of sleep coming from her husband. Loretta knew his routine like clockwork so when she came out of the laundry room she went to the stack of new mail he'd picked up earlier and thumbed through the envelopes.

"Hey Honey, how was your day?"

"It was O.K., how was yours?" he asked with a smile.

"Just fine," she answered. "I've still got a few more errands to run so I'll be back a little later. She went back to the counter to get her purse. "You know you have a FedEx package in here."

"Oh, yes, I forgot about that. I meant to pick that up during the week. Deacon Johnson gave me the sticker that was left on the church door."

"I'm surprised he didn't go pick it up for you."

"You know he wanted to but I had to personally sign for it. So I went on up there. There was a pretty long line for a Saturday but it moved pretty quick."

"Well, it's probably important if someone sent you something through FedEx."

"Perhaps, but if it was that important they should have called me and let me know they were sending something, so I'd be looking out for it. I meant to open it earlier but I'll get to it."

"Well, whoever sent you this doesn't know that much about our church," she chuckled looking at the big envelope. "They have on here to deliver first thing in the morning. On a business day? There's nobody at the church. They must not know that most small churches don't have anyone on staff during the week. But we'll get there," she shot him an optimistic look.

"Here you go," she said, handing it to him. Then she rubbed his head, running her fingers through his salt and pepper hair, then leaned down and kissed him on the cheek. "Alright, I'm gone."

"O.K., Dear." Pastor David looked at the return address on the envelope, sighed as his mind wondered what news, probably negative, this mail would bring, then put it back down on the arm of the chair and turned the channel just as his wife turned the key to lock the front door as she left the house.

Thirty minutes later, he was startled awake by a loud T.V. commercial and decided to get up and shake the drowsiness away. As he started for the kitchen for something cold to drink, the envelope fell from the chair arm to the floor.

"Alright, let's see what this is," he resigned.

He sat back down but this time, closer to the edge, so he wouldn't be too comfortable. He pulled the thin tab at the top. Opening the big envelope, he reached in and pulled out a smaller envelope. He set the now empty one to the side and opening the smaller envelope, he pulled out a folded piece of paper that had yet another smaller envelope stapled to the back of it. He opened the paper to find a letter.

Dear Pastor Wright. As his eyes intently read the thoughtful words expressed in the encouraging letter, his heart danced with delight. He glanced at the bottom of the letter for the name but it ended, *Most sincerely, Anonymous.* "O.K., that's interesting. You don't want me to know who you are. Hmmm." He reached down and picked up the envelope and looked at the senders address. Out of state and no name of a person and the company name listed looked like an acronym. Those few letters could stand for anything, but there was a phone number, if it was accurate. And the area code definitely wasn't local. "Well, they surely went through a lot of trouble to make themselves unknown. O.K. Lord." So his eyes went back up to the letter where his finger marked his place and he continued reading.

These were the types of letters that made anyone soar. His ministry had been a blessing to someone, and that was what it was all about. Whoever wrote the letter didn't make it clear whether they were a member of his church currently or in the past, or if they had just heard of the great work his church had done in the community. They mentioned some of the community outreach the church had implemented over the years, like the Back-To-School clothes and school supply giveaways, and the whole Thanksgiving dinners complete with fried turkeys, that the brothers cooked right there in the church parking lot very early on Thanksgiving mornings, and hand delivered to needy families. The letter even mentioned the church's generosity to the neighborhood children during Vacation Bible School.

Whoever wrote this knew a lot about the church but Pastor David still wasn't sure if it was a member or not because those events were not a secret. They weren't something that only the members would know. Vacation Bible School and the Back-To-School giveaways were always shared through social media and the Thanksgiving dinners were shared by word of mouth. What the letter didn't include were the small scale outreaches that took place on a regular basis at the church, like the visits to the nursing home, and the times during Christmas when they had contacted the nearby school asking them to provide the name and phone number of a few struggling families so that they could bless them during Christmas.

Pastor thought maybe they weren't members but could possibly be friends of one of the members or someone who had just liked their Facebook page or stumbled on their website and kept up with the church ministry. Either way, he was very pleased that someone, anyone would take the time to write this encouraging letter. It was another confirmation that their church was doing the right things. They were making a difference. They were actually doing ministry. That is one thing Pastor David always stressed to his leadership team and to the members. Everyone knew that Pastor was not interested in doing church work, but doing the work of the church, and everyone who spent any length of time there knew the difference.

After reading the body of the letter, past the closing, there was another entry. His eyes went to the very bottom of the paper where it read, "Pastor, please accept this monetary donation to the church, and may God continue to give you wisdom as to how to use it to continue to be a blessing. God is truly awesome!"

"That He is indeed!" Pastor exclaimed and stood as if he were in church, hollering back after someone asked, *"Can I get a witness?"* "A donation, that's so nice. Father, bless this person whomever they are, for taking the time out to write this to me. This has truly made my day." And tearing away the envelope that was stapled to the back of the letter, he held it up to heaven and prayed again, "Lord, bless this donation, whatever the amount. Let this seed flourish, and be placed in good ground. Let it bless our church so that we can continue to be a blessing to the body of Christ. Father, bless the donor beyond measure. Bless them in every aspect. Let there be no lack in their lives. Rebuke the devourer and multiply their blessings, in Jesus' name, Amen." He opened the envelope and pulled out a check.

"Jesus!" he screamed.

His knees buckled under the weight of the shock. He grabbed hold of the chair for support. He stared at the check in disbelief. "Oh, Lord." He counted all the zeros. He read each part of the check again like he was a child learning to read for the first time, sounding out each word as if it was the first time he had seen it.

"Two...hun...dred...thouuuu...sssaaannd...doll llarrrssss.

Twoooo...hunnnn...dddrreed...thoussaannd...dollar rsss? Two hundred thousand dollars!!!! Aaaahhhhh!!!! Jesus! Jesus! Jesus!!" He broke out in a straight-up sanctified, holy-ghost dance, shout, and praise break!

He danced, and danced for a long time, crying, balling, wailing, praying, falling to the ground, tossing back and forth, and jumping back up. "Oh, God!" He violently shook his head back and forth in utter amazement. Then, he started all over again.

Finally, after tiring himself out with his undignified praise, he swallowed hard under his heavy breathing. "Wait until I tell the church!"

Chapter 13

Tithes

EVERYONE FROM THE lottery pool gathered in the living room of Frank and Laura, catching up on things and encouraging each other to stick to the plan they all had previously agreed on.

"Mija," Maria speaking to Tammy fondly, "how are you doing it? It's hard enough making decisions as a couple using two heads, bouncing ideas off of one another and having someone to hold you accountable to your plans. Honey, how are you doing it alone?"

"I might be by myself, but I'm not alone. I lean on God's wisdom and He helps me. And I know I have you guys if I have a question, need advice, or get stomped by something."

"That's right," Maria assured her as Amanda nodded in agreement.

"That's true, but that's not the only person you've been leaning on," Frank teased.

"Yes, girl who is that young man you've been sitting next to at church?" Laura asked.

"His name is Jerome," Tammy tried to avoid blushing but failed.

"Uh, huh!" Craig blurted like he'd uncovered a secret.

"You two have been together for a while, it looks serious," Laura chimed.

"It kind of is," Tammy said reluctantly.

"Wow, it must be difficult having all that money and dating someone. There must be a million things running through your mind," Maria said.

"Yes, I have to watch what I do for him. I have to be careful about the kind of gifts I buy him, how often we eat out…it's pretty strange having to hold back."

"So what do you do?" Jorge asked.

"I just live on what I make and forget I even have the money. If this is going to work, I want it to work on what I make and I want to make sure he loves me for me."

"That's wise," Frank complimented.

"You guys are blessed to have each other and be married already," Tammy directed to everyone. Don glanced at Janet as she lowered her gaze and turned back to Tammy, who continues. "You already love each other for who you are. I've got to be careful and make sure he's not here because of what I have or what I can give him." She paused. "If he is the one, should I get a prenup?"

"Yes!" the room answered almost in unison. Everyone, including Tammy, laughed.

"Let's say he is the one," Jorge leaned in, "when are you going to tell him about the money?"

"Maybe after we've been married for about five years," Tammy thought out loud.

"Whoa!" Jorge sat up.

"No, uh unnn," Craig said. "I'd be mad as hell."

"Tammy, that is a long time," Laura said.

"Why so long?" Maria asked.

"Well, I don't know, three years?" Tammy threw her hands up. "I hear all these stories about how people change after they get married. I just want to make sure I don't make a mistake and later down the road find out he's not what he's portraying himself to be."

"Would you do that to me?" Craig asked Amanda.

"I don't know, but she has a point," Amanda answered back.

"Well, what would you do?" Tammy asked Craig.

"Oooh, one, maybe two years, that's it."

"I'd want to know right after I say 'I do,'" Frank chimed in.

"We can say what we would do but we really don't know because we're not in the situation," Laura added.

"But definitely not until you're already married," Frank advised.

"Of course," Tammy shook her head.

"But the sooner the better, so you can start living your life to the fullest and enjoying this tremendous blessing together. You get to experience the joy of picking who you want to bless, whatever charity God lays on your heart. Frank and I have had some real good conversations about that and it's so much fun," Laura said.

"Speaking of giving, Laura and I have already given to the church, well the tithes anyway," Frank informed everyone.

"You know I've been meaning to ask how you all plan on paying your tithes," Tammy surveyed the room. "You can't just put two hundred thousand dollars in the offering plate. Can you imagine the look on the deacon's face when he sees that check!" *Tammy imagined some of the deacons' expressions as they would pick up the cashier's check and read all of those zero's.* "One would start stuttering, the other might faint, and eventually the whole church would know that one of their own members had given the donation."

"We did ours anonymously and mailed it to the pastor directly," Frank responded.

"Wait a minute," Don interjected after calculating in his head. "Tammy, after taxes are taken out, the tithe is less than two hundred thousand dollars."

"Well, you're supposed to tithe off of the gross, the bigger number, not the net," Laura informed.

"Says who?" Don asked.

"It's in the Bible."

"Where?"

"Really?" Laura's forehead creased.

"Yeah, man, we do everything like that, our bonus checks from work, tax returns, any money that we get," Frank reported.

"Jorge, how do y'all do it?" Craig asked.

"We do the same thing but Maria and I decided to use that money to start a ministry."

"What? You mean you've been called to preach?" Craig asked.

"No, it's just we see the need of so many in our culture who are trying to come to America but can't afford it and this money will go a long way."

"But it's your tithes, you can't just use it at your discretion, even though it's a noble cause. It's not yours, it belongs to the church," Laura said.

"The people of our country are very poor, they live like peasants even compared to the poor in America. And they are facing grave danger, urgent life-threatening situations. We believe the Lord has blessed us with this money to help them, not to give it to build a bigger church building or provide laptops or something. We're talking about life and death situations," Jorge said.

"Don't get me wrong, we're going to give the church an offering, but this is something we won, it's not earnings, so we really don't have to give ten percent," Maria added.

"Oooh, I don't know about that Maria," Janet spoke up, "but I want to get you guys' opinion on something similar. What if we split our tithes between different churches? There are a couple of other churches that this money would really be a blessing to. I mean if we all gave our ten percent, that's one hundred thousand going to just one church, when we could bless so many other churches as well."

"I can't believe what I'm hearing," Laura said. "You haven't been getting your nourishment from a couple of other churches. You've been spiritually fed by one church. And Don, Pastor taught on giving the whole tithe and first fruits. I'm going to get the Bible so you can read it for yourself."

As Laura left the room, the conversation continued.

"I feel like since you were blessed with the money while going to our church, that's where your tithes should go," Tammy concluded.

"I agree with that," Frank added, "if you want to give to other churches, or other ministries and charities, give a donation but don't take away from the tenth that belongs to our church."

Amanda chimed in, "And whatever you do, make it anonymous. We gave some money to a charity here in town, just one time, and ever since then they've been sending us requests in the mail. We gave what, twenty or thirty dollars?" Amanda asked Craig. Nodding in agreement, Craig finishes, "And they've been asking ever since. That's been over three years. Just imagine what would happen if you gave like a thousand!"

"Good point. We know too well about that," Frank said.

"So tell us more about your ministry, Jorge," Craig prompted.

"Well, we are very excited. We're partnering with predominantly Hispanic churches and we help with finding housing, buying bus tickets to get family members into the states, helping with the paperwork to get work visas, and filling out residence applications. You name it, we do it, whatever assistance is needed."

"That's nice, sounds like you're helping a lot of people," Tammy said.

"So are you guys leaving our church?" Frank questioned.

Jorge and Maria looked at each other. "We haven't made a final decision but we're leaning that way."

The room grew silent at the thought of such good friends leaving the church that they've all been attending for so long.

Laura's re-entrance broke the awkward silence.

"Alright, I found my notes. I'll just read a few. In Malachi 3:8 it says we're robbing God with our tithes and offerings and to bring the whole tithe into the storehouse. It started in Gen 28:22 when Abram made an oath to give a tenth to Melchizedek the priest. And Proverbs 3:9 talks about honoring the Lord with your wealth and giving him the first fruits." No one spoke but a few heads nodded in agreement. "I'm just putting it out there, you have to decide what you're going to do," Laura concluded.

Laura sensed something was wrong. "What's the matter? What did I miss?"

No one wanted to speak Jorge and Maria's likely departure into the atmosphere so Frank simply responded, "I'll tell you later."

"Why don't we call it a night?" he somberly concluded to the group. And on that note, everyone slowly said their good-bye's, giving Jorge and Maria extra attention, and left for their homes.

Chapter 14

The One

TAMMY SPOKE SOFTLY, "I can't wait to see you. I really miss you." She had finally come to grips with what Jerome was trying to get her to see when telling her he didn't want her buying her own meals anymore. She had come to the conclusion that this issue was reasonable for her to flex on. The conversation with her dad helped as well. She reached out to him because she wanted to hear the opinion of the man closest to her. She was able to get her father's perspective, and he agreed with Jerome. She didn't consult her father about much, but he was good for giving advice on men and their motives. He could always spot a phony. And out of all the things he did wrong in his own marriage, he wanted the best for his daughter, so he told her what to watch out for in men and how to tell the men from the boys.

"Me too, I've been thinking about you all day," Jerome's eyes widened because he forgot who was sitting in the car with him.

Smiling on the other end, Tammy reluctantly brought the conversation to a close as she said, "Bye."

"Later," Jerome ended the conversation as he normally did, and hung up his cell phone.

"Man, she's got your nose wide open," Larry joked.

"Yeah, I really like her," Jerome looked at his friend in earnest as they made their way to the local gym to lift weights.

Jerome and Larry were friends since high school and had recently come across each other again while exercising. Now they tried to meet up all the time and serve as accountability partners to be consistent in their exercise regime. They had been football teammates so they had spent quite a bit of time together on and off the field. Larry hadn't been the star athlete in school but he was a consistent player who worked hard. Larry chose to pursue an engineering degree in college but Jerome never went. He didn't think college was for him, and instead chose to pick up a trade that held his passion, building. Larry was detailed and Jerome valued his take on things so he started a conversation. "Larry, I want to ask your opinion about something."

"Alright."

"It's about Tammy. Well…she sure does ask a lot of questions."

"Like what?"

"She wants to know my plan, where I see myself in five years. She wants to know how much money I make. And check this out, she even wants to see my credit report."

"Really?"

"Yeah, Man and I haven't even asked her to marry me."

"Is she a gold digger?" Larry asked without hesitation.

"No, she's not the type, but there's something she's not telling me. I just can't figure it out."

"Well, just ask her what's going on with all the questions." Larry thought some more, "She answers those same questions herself, that she asks you, right?"

"You know, I don't even ask her anything. I don't care about none of that," Jerome answered flatly.

"Jerome," Larry warned, "whatever question you answer from her, you should turn around and ask her the same question and see what she has to say. Don't just listen to what she says either, pay attention to how she answers, so you can see where she's coming from."

"Well she does volunteer the answers to the same questions she asks me, but she wonders why I don't ask *her*."

"Listen man, you need to get your head out of the clouds and pay attention to what's going on. You already sense something isn't right so you need to follow-up on that," Larry insisted.

As Jerome pulls up to the front entrance of the fitness center, he tells Larry to go on ahead inside while he parks the car and makes a phone call. After Larry shut the passenger door, Jerome looked for a parking spot. He wasn't sure he agreed with Larry or not so after putting the car in park, he picked up his phone to call his sister Barbara.

"Hey!" Barbara answered the phone excited to hear her brother's voice.

"Hey big sis," Jerome said lovingly. "I've got to ask you something."

"O.K."

"Well, Tammy keeps asking me a lot of questions and I just want to get your point of view."

"O.K. Like what?"

"Uh…" He somehow seemed embarrassed to tell her. "Like how much money I make, what my plans are; she even wanted to see my credit report."

"Hmmm, did she tell you her plans and show you her credit report?"

"Yes."

"O.K. then. She wants to make sure she's not marrying a dead beat. Everything she asks of you, she's willing to give right?"

"Yes, everything, but I haven't asked her to marry me."

"Boy, stop. Everyone knows where this is going. She's all you ever talk about and that's never happened with anyone else you've dated. Tammy's smart, she doesn't want just anybody. She's thinking about the future and wants to be on the same page with you. She wants to make sure you actually are going somewhere. She's a strong woman with a good head on her shoulders, don't be taken aback by that. That's a good thing, Jerome," Barbara assures him.

"Alright, O.K. Thanks. I'll talk to you later."

"O.K., Baby boy."

"Stop, Barbara. You know I hate that."

"Bye, boy!" Barbara giggled as she hung up.

"Lord," Jerome prayed, "I don't know what Tammy's not telling me, but I love her. So if there's something wrong, please show me." He smiled as he thought of her again and exited his car.

***

Don and Janet walked into the counselor's office after meeting in the parking lot. They drove separately today, as they had done before. Janet's heart wasn't into it, because her mind was already made up. She was just going through the motions, meeting Don again for their marriage counseling sessions. It would take a miracle for her husband to change, and she wasn't holding her breath.

Arriving early, they sat in the waiting area for a few moments. Janet didn't want to talk to Don so she quickly grabbed a magazine from the selection on the coffee table and thumbed through, biding time until they were called in. Don looked around the room. It still intrigued him because it didn't look like what he had first imagined. It looked more like someone's living room than an office waiting room. The décor was sofas with pillows and lazy-boy chairs, instead of chairs that made you sit straight up, with soft lighting and curtains draping the windows versus mini blinds. All designed, he assumed, to make couples feel more comfortable telling all their business. The faint footsteps on the carpet pulled him out of his trance.

"Nice to see you two again," Mr. Collins stated, signaling to them it was now time. As they walked into the room, he started again. "OK, let's get right down to it. Janet, as you know, this session is devoted solely to the issues you have with your husband. I'm sure you did your homework?" he stated as a question.

"Yes," Janet replied. One thing both she and Don appreciated about their counselor was his efficiency. He didn't waste time on small talk which was a plus since he charged one hundred and fifty dollars an hour. Of course they could afford to spend the money but neither one of them wanted to be taken advantage of by someone who deliberately prolonged meaningless conversation, just to pad their own pockets.

"Alright, I want you to read each item listed one by one. So read each issue, then explain in detail what you mean. You can give examples if you think it will help Don understand."

"O.K." She hesitated and looked at her paper, still uncomfortable airing out their dirty laundry to a stranger. "He's so negative. It seems like he comes home looking for something to criticize. And if you're always looking for something, you'll find it. No matter how nice the house looks, he'll find the one thing that's wrong. The problem that I have with that is that he hardly does any work in the house. I do mostly all the cleaning. I do the laundry, the..." she cuts it short. "The only thing he does is cook, on occasion, sometimes wash the dishes, and the yard work. And I do those as well, except for the yard. And he only sees the stuff *I* do wrong, never what he does."

"Alright, go to the next one," Mr. Collins instructed.

"I don't feel cherished. I feel like I'm just there. He comes home and he'll be talking on the phone and he'll just nod at me. When we were first married I used to kiss him when he came home; I used to kiss him whenever. Now he pushes me away and tells me he's doing something."

"Because you do it right in the middle of what I'm doing," Don explained.

Janet shot her eyes at Don, "You can't stop for two seconds to kiss me? I feel like he's taking advantage of me," Janet tells the counselor, not giving Don a chance to respond to her rhetorical question.

"He doesn't show me any affection until he wants to have sex. This has been a problem throughout our marriage and he uses the excuse that he doesn't know how. But that's not true because he did it while we were dating. Now, if I were withholding sex from him, then he'd have a problem.

I keep telling him, affection is a basic need for a woman, just like sex is for a man."

Janet sighed and looked at her husband in disgust and frustration then looked down at her paper and wondered if she should continue.

"You know, I sound like a broken record. I'm so tired of going through the same thing over and over again." She looked at her husband. "Everything on this paper, you already know. I've told you several times."

"Janet, please keep going," the counselor urged.

"Both of us learned," she continued more calmly, "that the husband is supposed to be the priest, protector, and provider of his home. He won't even read the Bible with me. When I ask him to pray together, he tells *me* to pray and he just listens and says amen. What kind of leadership is that? If he is going to be the priest, *he* should be the one initiating, *he* should be the one setting the tone of our spiritual walk in *our* home, not me. I'm tired of having to be the one. That's not my role."

"You know what, I can't do this," Janet said plainly. "This is embarrassing." She leaned over to get her purse off of the floor and stood.

"Janet, please wait," Mr. Collins pleaded.

"I'm sorry, I just can't," she told the counselor, then glanced at her husband and walked out the door.

Chapter 15

Sunday Morning

LAURA AND FRANK walked into the church building on Sunday morning, excited about what their tithes on the winnings could do for the ministry. As they stood in the vestibule waiting for the opening prayer to end, Laura imagined all the projects that could be taken care of with just her and Frank's tithes on the winnings. She would make the women's bathroom a top priority, transforming it into a spacious oasis complete with a sitting lounge area and the installation of more bathroom stalls and a wall-to-wall mirror.

She surveyed the vestibule and noted that a nicer light fixture could be found to replace the current one and it wouldn't hurt to get new front doors as well. She tilted her head back down and paid attention to the prayer on the other side of the double doors. Laura could see Maria and Jorge through the window but wasn't in the position to see who else from the pool was already there.

The prayer was now over and the ushers opened the doors to let the parishioners in. Frank and Laura took their seats as the pastor walked into the sanctuary. They watched him intently. His face was full of gladness and there was a pep in his step. During the service, they tried to focus on the sermon and all the other parts of the service but they were anticipating what, if anything, the pastor may say to the congregation about the anonymous gift. Laura looked around for people in the congregation that she and Frank could bless. A single mother of three on row eight, a gentleman who Frank had mentioned had been out of work for two months on the third row, a young girl, who everyone found out is gifted at acting when she starred in the church play, who could benefit from acting lessons sitting in the choir stand.

There were so many needs that people seemed to have and Laura could justify a need with every face she saw. *How do you choose?* That was the question Laura contemplated in her mind. *If we help everybody, there'll be no money left for us to enjoy,* Laura thought. *These are some good people,* her mind continued, *I wonder if I can convince everybody in the lotto pool to pitch in enough to give every member five thousand dollars? I'd have to get the membership list. Wait, there's so many people who I hardly see anymore.* Her eyes surveyed the congregation. *How do you decide if they're really a member or have just left and didn't tell the pastor they've moved their membership? The word is going to get out no matter how many times you say 'don't say anything' or 'don't tell anybody' and then there will be people coming back saying they didn't get anything, that they haven't been here because they work on Sunday or whatever. And what about the many people who will just start showing up with all kinds of sad stories that they've just conjured up to prey on the church?* Laura looked at the pulpit. *I don't want to cause any confusion or heartache to the church. Wow, this is more difficult than I expected.* She crossed her arms.

Immediately after the announcements were read, the pastor stood and took the podium. *O.K., this may be it,* Frank thought, looking at Laura.

Late the night before, Laura sent the pool members a text suggesting they be more cautious this Sunday since she and Frank had just given their tithes on the lotto winning and the pastor was bound to say something. Laura didn't want any of them to make any obvious glances at one another no matter what the pastor may or may not say. She didn't want the pastor to notice anything and she surely didn't want anyone in the congregation to make any assumptions or jump to conclusions.

The pastor looked over the congregation for a long time without saying a word. Laura's heart began to beat faster. His glance seemed to be searching the faces of those in attendance. *Stay calm. Don't give yourself away. No sudden movements.* Laura swallowed hard. *Lord, please don't show him.* She knew anything was possible and if her pastor had asked God to show him who had given the money, it was possible that God would grant his request. Pastor David's eyes fell on her. She willed herself not to blink or break his gaze. *Lord, no.* She felt like she was in a police line-up, guilty, but hoping not to be pointed out by the witness on the other side of the glass. He only locked on her eyes for a few seconds but it only takes that long to pick up on something awry.

He moved his glance to someone else, Laura wondered what the other pool members were doing. What were their demeanors? She dared not look to any of them. The silence was uncomfortable but almost hopeful because Pastor had such warmth in his eyes and a smile on his face, even though he wasn't physically smiling, his face was happy. There was no denying that. It seemed like he was reminiscing. "God is so good," his words broke the silence.

"Amen," the congregation answered in unison.

"All the time," a few said, almost on cue.

"I'm so excited and humbled about what has happened." He talked slowly and paused as if he was overwhelmed or just carefully contemplating every single word. "God has placed this ministry on someone's heart, and they have blessed it. God has given us a tremendous blessing and I want to be a good steward of it."

"Alright!" someone shouted.

"Bless His name!" another exclaimed.

"It never occurred to me until now that this donor may be here this morning. They gave anonymously y'all so don't even ask me," he informed the congregation. "To the very kind, generous, thoughtful donor, I thank God for you." His eyes panned the congregation further. "Thank you for thinking of this ministry. I don't know why, out of all the churches you could have blessed, you chose this one. Only God could have placed us on your heart, and I don't even have the words to express my gratitude to you." He paused to compose himself from a shaky voice about to burst forth with tears. "Again, thank you so much."

"Uh uhmm," he cleared his throat as if to stop the tears and make his voice cooperate. "I've thought about how to approach this. I want to honor this gift. I thought about doing a church-giving drive, where I tell you that throughout the next two months, whatever you give will be matched dollar for dollar by a generous donor, but that wouldn't really be true because they've already given the money. I also thought about giving a portion of this money to *you*; all the members, *(he motioned with his hands)* but how?

Do I pick a Sunday and say 'calling all members I need everyone to be at church for a special event; members only; if you don't come on that day to get the blessing God has for you, you won't be able to get it later?" he questioned.

"Say it, say it," a voice from the front called out.

"How would I keep it quiet; keep it from being publicized? The word would get out and everyone in the city would be here. Then I thought about just picking a Sunday and whoever God chooses to be here that Sunday, member or not, gets the blessing. You know, kind of like casting lots. Do I have any bible readers in here?"

"Alright Pastor," someone yelled out.

"If I do that, how do I go about giving it to you once you get here? Do I frisk everybody at the door by asking that all cell phones be left up front in a box? Because I don't want any publicity, and no YouTube videos floating around on the internet. And please, I hope nobody's recording me now." He lowered his head and cut his eyes around the sanctuary. "Do I put money in envelopes and put them under every seat in the sanctuary? As soon as I announce something like that, I'd have people jumping out of the stands up there *(he pointed to the balcony)*, jumping onto the chandeliers to get closer to the ground, to snatch up the envelopes under any empty seats. People would be climbing down the curtains like animals…"

Laughter trickled out of a few people.

"See look at that, some of you are already reaching under you seats just to check."

More laughter broke out.

"How do you use this money without making our ministry a circus? No matter how I do it, or how much is given, you won't satisfy everyone, even when you're giving them money they didn't expect."

"You're right, Reverend."

"That's the truth," an older woman waved her hand.

"If you're not careful you can create a rift in the church. I want this gift to bless this ministry and this community. I want it to be a blessing and not a hindrance. You know I've been praying too. So I've decided, unless the Lord tells me otherwise, to do a couple things right now. We're going to stay the course and expedite the building of the children's facility. And we *are* going to conduct a giving drive. For the next two months I want you to give like never before. Why you ask? I want you to be blessed. This donation came from one source but look around. Look at the people here. There are many of us. If we focus, all of us, we can do great things, together. We should rededicate our commitment in regards to giving. Some of us can do more than what we've been doing. Yes, we should purpose in our hearts what we should give, I've taught on that. So what is your heart saying? And some of you have stopped tithing and need to make that right with God and start back today. You might be thinking, 'why do we need to give more when someone else already gave a lot' but what you don't understand is that they will be blessed by *their* gift, God will bless you by *your* gift. I'm talking tithes *and* offerings here. God's not going to bless you on *my* obedience, he blesses you for your own obedience. Don't get quiet on me now."

"Alright, preacher."

"Tell it!"

"Make it plain."

A variety of exclamations came from the choir stand all the way to the balcony.

"I'm not fussing, please don't get me wrong. This is a happy day! God has shown himself mighty! I want us to stretch our faith. Amen?"

Excitement jumped from person to person all around the sanctuary. People started standing up in the pulpit, ladies were hugging each other in the choir stand and men were slapping each other hi-fives. Even the musician got up from his stool and started playing some shouting music.

"Amen! Amen!" the church erupted with praise.

Chapter 16

The Ex

CRAIG'S PHONE RANG and he reached to see who it was. He frowned and considered his options. He had already sent her to voicemail twice the last few days and he hadn't bothered to listen to her messages. Thinking he might as well get this over with, he clicked the green icon.

"Yes, Gloria."

"Well, hello to you too. I left you a message to call me back."

"I've been so busy, I haven't even listened to them. What is it?"

"Josh says you're paying for him to go to college."

"Yes, and?"

"Why didn't you tell me?"

"This is for Josh. It has nothing to do with you."

"As long as he's living under my roof, if it concerns him, it concerns me too."

It won't be long if I have anything to do with it, Craig thought. "All those times you took me back to court to ask for an increase in child support, you didn't call me to discuss anything. I had to find out from the courts and now you want me to tell *you* something. I don't have to tell you anything. This is between me and Josh."

"I don't want you getting his hopes up for nothing. If you say you're going to pay for it then I expect you to come through."

"At least I'm giving him hope. What have you been teaching him?"

"What do you mean by that?"

"He can't make a life for himself working at a fast food restaurant. He has no plan for his future—"

"I'm not his only parent. You didn't teach him anything either."

"That's your fault?"

"Excuse me?"

"You were too busy trying to keep him away from me; trying to get back at me for whatever, but all you did is hurt our son. How many times did I call you asking to see him and you said he was busy, couldn't leave or told me he wanted to be with his friends? You should have been a mother and made him come with me so I can teach him something. A man needs his father."

"If you're such a man you could've made him come with you. He didn't want to."

"Gloria, how do you think he would even want to come with me when you spend every waking moment talking bad about me? Y'all wouldn't even answer the phone when I would call and check on—"

"I called you many times."

"Gloria, the only time you would call is when you wanted me to discipline him. That's it. Now, you tell me how can I discipline my son when you won't even let me have a relationship with him? Kids don't respond to that. All you wanted me to do is fix problems that you created. And every time things got better between you and him, you shut me out again, like I didn't even exist. You thought you were hurting me, well you did I'll admit that, but Josh is the one who suffered the most."

"If you aren't man enough to get him to want to see you that's your problem."

Craig closed his eyes. He was upset at himself for even going down this road with a woman who refused to see past her own selfishness. Why would he bring up the past when he knew she was a lost cause? He would have to make the most of whatever time he now had with Josh and end this pointless conversation with his mother by discussing the topic at hand, his education.

"About college, he says you're not even helping with anything."

"I can't afford to."

"What in the world did you do with all that money over the years?"

"I spent it raising your son."

Now he's my son, only when it's convenient for you, Craig shook his head. "You didn't save anything for his college?"

"No, did you?"

"Gloria, you were getting money from me every paycheck. You should have saved some of it for his future. You spent every dime didn't you?"

"He has a roof over his head, food and clothes...yes I spent it on life. He's here isn't he?"

More wasted time, Craig thought. "Is that all you called for? I've got to go?"

"Well, bye then." And as quickly as she had intruded his day, she exited.

Chapter 17

News Break

CRAIG AND AMANDA sat on the couch, cuddled up as they finished watching a movie. As Craig switched back to T.V. mode they cut into a news cast already in progress.

"...on FM 1960 at *this* convenience store, one lucky winner won ten million dollars, and that means a healthy check for the owners of this establishment as well."

Amanda abruptly sat up to the edge of her seat. "That's where Laura bought the tickets. That's our ticket they're talking about."

"I hope no one puts two and two together," Craig's mind went into overdrive.

"Well, what if someone from church figures it out? With the donation, and now this news about the win..." Amanda kept watching.

"With the corner store being that close to the church, I don't know," Craig said.

"Laura," Amanda had quickly dialed her number and put her on speakerphone, "Are you watching the news?"

"Yes, I saw it," Laura sighed. "You know I normally buy the tickets from a store close to my job but that day I got off work late and bought them on my way to bible study. Wow! Of all days, it had to be that one."

"You think somebody will figure it out?" Amanda probed.

"No, I don't think so. Well, with pastor just talking about the donation, it will be fresh on people's minds, and then if they watch this they may wonder, but what else would they have to go on? We've been careful about everything so I don't see how," Laura figured.

"O.K. Well, we'll see."

"Surely not," Craig rethought. Millions of people live in Houston. There's no way."

"Alright, you heard him. I guess we'll talk to you later."

"Bye."

Laura looked at Frank who was now at the kitchen table.

"What, someone's getting worked up over the news?" Frank asked.

"It's a little concerning. It's just bad timing with…"

"With Pastor talking about it over the pulpit," Frank interjected.

"It's strange. I was excited and wondered what he would say and how he would say it and how the congregation would react. But now—"

"Now you wonder if he should have said anything at all."

"Yes! I know he was excited and I don't blame him but when he told everyone not to record, I just had a weird feeling. People can be so defiant. I wouldn't be surprised if someone started recording just because he said not to."

She looked at Frank with hopeful eyes. "But we're a family of believers right? No one would do anything spiteful or hateful with that information, right?"

"Right," Frank slowly repeated, not even trying to convince her.

"More importantly, with my parents inviting all of us over to dinner tomorrow night; I know they're going to talk about the money and the letter we sent them. If they saw this," Laura pointed to the T.V. screen, "they may know we had something to do with it."

"Why us, why can't it be Nell?" Frank asked.

"Nell would have just came out and told them. She wouldn't miss taking credit for something like that."

"Well, what about Maury? Never mind," Frank shook his head emphatically. "Don't even answer that. Well, this ought to be interesting."

"I can't wait," Laura rolled her eyes.

Chapter 18

Committed

JEROME AND TAMMY walked through the door of her apartment after returning from a night on the town. He set his keys on the counter.

"I had a wonderful time. It was so beautiful."

"I'm glad you liked it."

Jerome was unusually quiet all evening. He didn't say much at all to the wait staff and kept fidgeting. She hoped he wasn't coming down with something. Her immune system was iron clad, being exposed to so much on a daily basis. Tammy never knew what ailment a patient may have, but she always tried to be careful since she knew at any time she could be a carrier. She wondered if she had made a bad judgement a few days ago when she came straight over to Jerome's apartment after work without first going home to take a shower. She would have to remember to be more careful.

Maybe Jerome didn't feel she appreciated all the effort he had put into the evening, so she made sure to point out the details now. "That was my first time at the Water Wall. It was breathtaking the way the sunset reflected off of the water, and the big oak trees. The walk there was really romantic too. And thank you for the warning about wearing comfortable shoes." She chuckled as she glanced down at her sandals. He didn't return the laugh but he did give her a half-hearted smile.

"I'm glad you enjoyed it. And that was my first time as well. I didn't know so many people would be there. It wouldn't have surprised me if we had seen a tour bus nearby."

Jerome walked Tammy to the living room and sat her down on the couch.

"And the water, wow, it's so powerful—"

Jerome nodded and sighed as he sat beside her. "And not as quiet and tranquil as you would expect. I didn't realize it would be hard for us to hear each other talk."

She hoped he didn't think she was complaining so she added, "Again, I thank you so much for a wonderful, memorable evening."

"You're more than welcome." He gave her an intense yet loving look. Tammy's chest started to pound and her cheeks filled with color. She briefly looked down, his gaze too powerful. She shifted her body. There was silence for a moment as he took in her beauty. He looked at the canvas of her face as if examining a rare porcelain doll, amazed by its craftsmanship and perfection. He gently caressed his hand against her cheek. He swallowed hard. Then he slowly started to speak, "Tammy, you know you have my heart. From the first moment that I saw you, I knew you would be a part of my life. I just wish I would have met you sooner."

Jerome paused for a moment and smiled. Then he continued, "I'd do anything for you. I always want you with me. I want to wake up to your face every morning and embrace you every night. Tammy Evelyn Chapman, will you marry me?" He opened up a small box he'd been carrying in his front pants pocket all night.

Tammy's eyes widened. She was now aware of why he had been acting strange all evening; why the romantic set up at the wall and his previous disappointment. He must have planned on asking her there but changed his mind, she wasn't sure if it was because of the noise or lack of privacy. "Yes. Yes, I will." Tammy smiled shyly and Jerome cradled her face with the palm of his hand, shaping his fingertips on the side of her neck and leaned in, embracing her with a long, deep kiss.

Tammy lay there in his arms for a long time, his lips gently kissing her forehead, then her hair, and squeezing her just enough, as if to assure his protection for her. Just before she was about to dose off, Jerome grabbed her hand. "Now, I want you to know, whatever happens, we'll be alright. I may not make a lot of money but whatever I have it's yours. O.K.?"

She shook her head in agreement.

He started playing with her fingers. "Now, what is it you're not telling me?" He let the question settle. "You've been asking questions here and there and I see the way you look at me, like you're wondering what kind of man I really am. So what is it? Lay it on me. Whatever it is, I can handle it."

Tammy looked at Jerome intently. *Oh my Lord I'm going to marry this man,* she thought. *What would be wrong if I told him? He just committed to me. If I tell him, I can stop all the charades and won't have to keep anything from him any longer.* Her mind raced. *But will that change things between us? I don't know how it would but it's possible. What am I doing? My emotions are getting the best of me. Just stick to the plan.* She wanted to tell him about her fortune but she knew she just couldn't until after they were married. And even after that she had planned to wait awhile longer. But one thing she had learned about Jerome during their courtship is that he's persistent. Tammy knew that she hadn't been able to get anything over on him; not that she had tried, it's just that he could tell when something was on her mind, he could sense even the slightest thing that may be bothering her. She had to tell him something though, or he wouldn't let up, even as gentle and as nonchalant as his question was.

She sat up, pushed past her fogginess and thought fast. "I was just so reluctant to start a relationship because I'm too trusting and I've been hurt before. I know I've asked you a lot of questions, and maybe I still do ask too many, I'm just being super cautious. I love you and I really hate the thought of being so vulnerable to your love because when I love I don't hold back. I'm too trusting, and the men in my past have taken advantage of that, so forgive me. I hope to get better and I thank you for your understanding thus far."

"There's no need to apologize for anything," Jerome assured her. "You can ask me all the questions you want, to make sure you're satisfied."

She leaned over and gave him another slow passionate kiss that she hoped would clear his mind so she could change the subject. It worked. Now she just had to remember to continue to focus on him and their relationship and forget she had won the money, for now.

Chapter 19

Family Affair

SITTING AROUND THE dinner table were Frank and Laura, Laura's parents, her sister Nell, and brother Maury. Maury was single again so he came alone and Nell's husband Paul was on another military tour so two chairs were removed and placed in the corners of the room so it felt cozier. Black placemats with gold embellishments adorned the cherry stained table. Matching them were napkin holders and charger plates that sat under the good china. Laura always liked seeing the lights of the chandelier reflecting off of the newly-polished wood and unto the wall paper that lined the bottom half of the walls, just below the crown moulding.

Laura's parents had really gone all out for this dinner. There was so much food. They had two meats; smothered pork chops and roast, over rice, mustard greens and sweet potatoes, purple hull peas, cornbread, and pasta salad, with honey-butter biscuits. Dessert was your choice of triple chocolate cake or pecan pie and to wash it all down was tea lemonade.

If the dining room set up didn't give away the reason they were there, the hefty dinner did. This was indeed a special occasion and Frank and Laura definitely knew why they were all here.

"Mamma, that was delicious," Maury said as he leaned over and kissed her on the forehead.

"Yes ma'am," Laura agreed as she picked up her mom's plate and headed for the kitchen.

Everyone started in on how great the meal was as the matriarch of the family smiled with satisfaction.

"I'm glad you all enjoyed it," Maggy said.

"Alright, y'all go ahead and take care of the dishes, because me and your mamma want to talk to you about something," Tom said.

"What is it, Daddy?" Nell asked, finishing the last of her biscuit.

"No, y'all go on and get finished first. We'll be in the living room," Tom reiterated.

Here we go, was the look Laura gave to Frank as she picked up his plate to return to the kitchen.

"I'll help," Frank said as he picked up some dishes from the table, eager to get the real purpose that they were all called over for dinner, out and over with.

"What's this talk about," Maury asked.

"Who knows," Laura answered, as she began the first of what she knew would be many bouts of acting, only this role would determine if she would continue to live an anonymous stress-free life. She had better make it a convincing performance.

"I hope they're not gonna go through some morbid stuff like burial plots and funeral arrangements," Nell said.

"Well, that is important. We're all gonna go one day and we need to know what their wishes are," Laura stated. Feeling a little more comfortable in her response, and in her performance to what seemed like the dress rehearsal right before a live Broadway show, she told herself to just act normal and forget about the money, just respond naturally.

"I'm with Nell, I don't want to even think about that sort of stuff," Maury said with disgust.

"Not talking about it doesn't stop it from happening, Maury. And talking about it doesn't make it happen. You know it's coming one day so at least we can be prepared," Laura shot back.

Frank kept silent and kept cleaning up. He saw no use in adding to this sibling discussion.

"Well if that's what it is, I may leave early. Whatever y'all decide, when the time comes, just let me know," Maury concluded, drying the last dish.

After about twenty minutes of everyone pitching in to wash and dry the dishes, wipe the table, and put things back in their places, Laura, Nell, and Maury walked from the kitchen to the living room in age order, like clockwork, just as they had many times before, growing up. Frank followed.

"Thank you for cleaning up," Maggy started.

"Of course, Mamma," Maury said as his siblings and Frank all chimed in something of the same sentiment.

"Well, Everybody," Tom slid his palms together back and forth, his grin filled his entire face.

He's too excited to be about to talk about death, Nell thought as she glanced at Maury.

Maury understood the meaning of her glance and shrugged his shoulders.

"We wanted to tell you all at the same time. And we don't even know how to explain it." Tom grabbed his wife's hand as if to urge her to help him tell it.

"Yes, I...it's so amazing...unbelievable," Maggy stammered.

"What?" Maury asked.

"Yeah, Mamma, what is it?" Nell smiled, catching the excitement.

"Daddy!" Laura faked, making sure she wasn't left out.

"Somebody paid off our house!" Tom shouted.

"What, no way! Mamma, that's unbelievable," Nell's eyes doubled in size.

Maggy started to cry as she had when she and Tom originally received the news.

"You've got to be kidding?" Maury stood up to shake his father's hand. "No stuff?" he added.

"That's great, wow!" Laura added.

"Father-n-law, that's fantastic," Frank added as he shook Mr. Robinson's hand then leaned over to give Maggy a kiss on the cheek.

"Oh my God. How? Who?" Nell asked the obvious questions.

"We don't know," Tom and Maggy simultaneously said.

Laura and Frank stole a quick uncomfortable look at each other.

"We have no idea. We just got this letter in the mail, well it came certified mail, saying that they wanted to bless us," Maggy stammered.

"They?" Nell asked.

"Well the person; I think it's one person," Maggy self-corrected.

"And they didn't say who they were or why?" Maury asked.

"No, and that's not all," Maggy smiled back at Tom, "they paid off our back taxes."

"Can you believe it!" Tom jumped in, exuberated.

"Wait a minute," Maury halted, "how would they know you have back taxes?"

"I don't know, we're probably in some sort of database or something," Tom reasoned.

"Maury's right, how would anybody know something like that?" Nell asked Laura.

"Maury's right, that is odd," Frank stated while giving Laura that I-told-you-so look.

"Wait, back up a minute," Maury said in contemplation. "Why would somebody pay this off?" Tom gave his son a dirty look.

"I mean umm," Maury quickly tried to clean up his statement, "why wouldn't they buy you a *bigger* home in a *nicer* neighborhood?"

"I don't need a bigger home," Maggy informed him, "that's just more to clean. And we've lived here for years. You grew up right here. We have history in this house. This is our home. And we like our neighborhood. No, it's not the best and it certainly isn't what it used to be when you all were small but we know all the neighbors and we look out for one another. It's like a community, well it's more like an extended family."

"And a bigger home means bigger bills," Tom added.

Maggy nodded in agreement.

"You don't just get a bigger, newer, anything just because," Laura scolded Maury. "What good would it be for Mom and Dad to get a house, even if it *is* free, if they can't afford the maintenance and upkeep?"

"That's true, Maury. Cause if somebody *gave* you a new Mercedes, you wouldn't even be able to afford to change a spark plug," Nell joked.

Everybody laughed as Maury nodded his head at Nell as if to say, *I'll get you back for that.*

"They also, well he or she also, gave us some spending money," Maggy's smile widened as she shook her shoulders in excitement.

131

"Man, y'all hit it big time." Maury said.

"How much?" Nell asked.

"Come on Nell, that's their business," Laura objected.

"Well, aren't y'all curious?" Nell looked back and forth to Maury and Laura.

"Enough for us to take a nice vacation and pay a little more bills," Tom answered, as he looked at Maggy and held her tight.

"That's so nice, I'm so excited for you!" Laura tried to keep them focused on the excitement.

"Hey, me too. And if you wanna drop a thousand my way, I sure could…"

"Maury!" Laura erupted, "That's their money, let them enjoy it."

"No disrespect. I'm not beggin' or even asking really, I just, you know, since they have so much, they might want to impart a few dollars from their new-found wealth on their *only* son."

Frank put his head down, remembering all the trouble his brother-n-law had given his parents. Maury had been in and out of every sales deal you could possibly imagine. He was always looking to make a big score on investments but nothing ever panned out. The problem was, he'd always come ask his parents for money to cover his next month's rent or whatever, because he kept chasing the next fantasy. That saying, 'If it's too good to be true, it probably is' never came across Maury's ears.

Maury was always looking for the next hustle, but no one really knew what he did for a living. He was the modern-day "Tommy" on the T.V. show Martin. Maury always had something going. He was eager to make something happen but he just didn't think things through. He rushed into too many deals and was either naïve or not equipped to handle the ins and outs of the industries he was pursuing.

Nell was unusually quiet, which was a gift to all assembled, considering most of the time she spoke, it was to point out something negative. But this time, even though her mouth was silent, her mind was working overtime. Laura looked at her, knowing whatever Nell was about to say next wasn't going to be good.

"A couple of things," Nell started. Whenever she led with that phrase, you'd better watch out because she was about to give you the "what for" or "hand you your hat" as the old folks would say. Nell studied law for a couple of years but switched over to nursing. Now she was about to make their parents' living room her own personal courtroom.

Laura knew she should have put in the letter, that they couldn't tell anyone but she didn't want to be too controlling and she knew that keeping a secret like that would be virtually impossible for her parents to do, a decision that she now regretted.

"Mamma, where's this letter?" Nell asked. "And do you know anyone that works for the government?"

"No."

"What's your point, Nell?" Laura asked.

"Just curious. Why would someone be so generous and how would they know such sensitive information? Mamma, do you talk about that stuff with any of your friends?"

"No, I don't think so, I'm pretty private."

"Daddy?"

"No, Nell."

"And who do you all hang around that has so much money that they can afford to give so much to you guys?" Nell interrogated.

"We don't *hang around* anybody," Tom said.

"Ha, you got that right," Maury laughed. Y'all don't do nothing but go to church and come home and wait for the next service," Maury chuckled loudly.

"Maury, don't start. That's what we choose to do. We enjoy it," Maggy said.

"But you don't have a life. You might as well move your furniture into the church so when you get up in the morning, all you have to do is get dressed and walk into the auditorium, you won't even have to drive. It'll save you so much time." Maggy's eyes narrowed and her lips tightened as she looked at her son. "I'm just playing mom, but I bet even the preacher gets tired of seeing you two," he added another jab.

"If you'd go more often, you'd know it's called the sanctuary, not an auditorium. And we do have a life, a pretty good one at that," Tom chastised.

"And they probably go so often because they're praying for you," Laura added.

"Wait a minute," Nell thought. "Who do you know at the church that's kind of well off?"

"What? I don't know. Nobody, that *I* know of," Maggy answered.

"You know what," Maury chimed. "I saw something on the news a couple days ago about somebody winning the lottery. They bought the ticket not too far from here at a gas station."

Nell milled over this information as if to see if it fit in the puzzle.

"But church folk don't play the lottery, do they? Because they know that Jesus, will make a way-a-aaaaaa, ye-es, he will-i-i-illll," Maury kidded as he sarcastically sung the line to an old standard church song.

At that moment, Laura was overjoyed that she and Frank didn't attend the same church as her parents or siblings because neither of them had heard their pastor's announcement.

"Mamma, are you gonna get the letter?" Nell pestered.

"Not now, no. Can you just enjoy this moment with us without trying to figure out everything. I'm just happy they, he, she, whomever, cared enough about me and your daddy, to bless us. They didn't put their name on the letter, so what. And I'm glad they didn't, or you'd probably be pestering them. God used them to bless us and that's that."

"But Mamma, aren't you curious?" Maury asked.

"Yes, of course I am, but that's the way they chose to do it and I'm fine with that. I just wish I could thank them...not give them the third degree." Maggy shot a disapproving look at Nell. "As a matter of fact, I'm not showing you the letter. If you get one, you can analyze yours, as for ours, that's our business." Maggy looked at Tom and then nodded her head an emphatic "now what" nod.

Tom looked at Nell and the rest of their children. "Well, you heard your mamma," and shook his head, forbidding anymore questions.

Laura was relieved. She knew Nell would go to great lengths just to find out who the benefactor was. She wouldn't be surprised if Nell wouldn't pull some strings and have someone in forensics analyze the paper for fingerprints, and she didn't even work in law enforcement. Laura was also very surprised that her mom was so satisfied with not knowing, she thought it would be her mother that would have asked all the questions, yet it was Nell doing all the digging. Just to make sure this didn't come up again,

Laura added, "I don't think we should say anything to anyone about this."

"Why?" Maury asked.

"Your response right there is the reason, Maury. Your response should have been, 'yeah, you're right.' I don't want this to get out and one of your hoodlum friends hits my mamma on the head thinking she's rolling in bank. And I don't want you *directed at Nell* "to start running your mouth and soon our relatives are calling Mamma asking her all these questions or asking Daddy for some money. Do you know how much stress that would put them through?"

"Laura's right," Tom interjected. "You three are the only ones we've told and are gonna tell, you too Frank, so let's leave it at that."

"What about *my* husband?" Nell asked, seeking the same privilege that Frank received.

"I'm sure you don't tell your husband everything that goes on while he's away," Maury added.

Nell gave him a look that would scare anybody, but she shut her mouth up. Laura didn't know if Maury had something on Nell or if he was finally making sense and she just didn't like it. Either way, it worked and that was good enough for Laura.

"Maury's right for a change," Tom said, "If we decide to tell him, that's our choice."

"On that note, it's time to go," Maury said. "Congratulations again, I really am happy for you. And thank you, Mamma, the food really was good as always," he stated as he gave her a kiss and his father a hand shake.

Following Maury's cue, Nell said her goodbye's and so did Frank and Laura.

After Frank and Laura got in their car, they just sat there for a moment in silence. Laura was so happy that her mom set things straight with everybody and Frank was just happy that it was over.

Chapter 20

Wise Women

TAMMY ARRIVED AT Jorge and Maria's home. She was excited yet fearful about Jerome proposing to her and she wanted, needed to get some advice from who she felt were wise women. She also had some concerns about what this meant as far as her portion of the lottery winnings. Not only how to make sure she didn't slip up and reveal anything to Jerome but she also remembered something in the contract that the lawyer added especially for her.

Tammy had a special circumstance, being the only one single in the pool. She had more requirements than the married couples because of it. The main thing she had agreed to do if she was ever to get married and wanted to tell her husband about the win, was he had to agree to keep the win a secret like everyone else had to. Jerome would have to sign an addendum to the contract and adhere to all the rules that everyone was already abiding by. And if they were to ever get a divorce, as was the stipulation for everyone else, they had to keep the secret or be subject to being sued by the trust.

Tammie had agreed to it all by signing her name. It made sense at the time, and still did, but now Tammy was faced with actually having to go through with it and she was concerned how Jerome would act. She didn't have to face that for quite some time though because she still didn't plan on telling him for a while after they were married. She didn't know if she would be able to keep her initial plans of waiting five years but however long it would be, she suspected it would still be a tough conversation.

Today though, she had other things on her mind. She was concerned that she and Jerome were moving too fast. And although she felt he was the one for her, she didn't know if she was being blinded by her love for him. She didn't want to make a mistake and regret it later. And there was something else.

She knew all the couples had given her sound advice, and knew the reasoning behind it but she just didn't think she could go through with it...the prenup. How could she do it? How do you just slip that into a conversation with someone you say you want to spend the rest of your life with? Jerome already thinks she doesn't fully trust him, even though she finally gave in and lets him buy her dinner. When she asks him to sign a prenup, if she has the nerve to actually do it, will it take him all the way back to square one? Tammy felt too much pressure and she couldn't talk to anyone else about it but her friends in the lottery pool, so she took a deep breath and pulled into the last space in the driveway.

Jorge and Maria's house was a picture of serenity. Pale yellow with white trim and a wrap-around porch with trees that hovered above and around it, seemingly protecting it, as if they knew how special the house was. Tammy could imagine Jorge and Maria spending many nights outside relaxing and allowing the white oversized swing to rock their concerns away as they watched the sun take another dip into the hues of dark orange and red ribbons that streaked the sky.

She rang the doorbell even though she could hear the high-pitched voices inside. Janet met her at the door with a hug. Tammy was greeted by hello's and well wishes all the way from the kitchen. She was escorted past the living room to where the lively bunch was congregated. Laura was seated around the kitchen table and Amanda was pouring a drink at the counter. Maria was busy taking a pan out of the oven and took her mittens off to embrace her.

"Oh, Mija! Congratulations. I am so happy for you." After the warm embrace she took Tammy's hand and in the same motion, she brought it up closer and added, "Let me see the ring. Oh, es muy bonita, Mija."

From the tone of her voice and mannerisms, everyone understood Maria's description of the ring being beautiful. Maria seemed to always speak more of her historical dialect when she was in her own home. The couple spoke it almost exclusively in their home, at least when they didn't have company, so the women were used to how she would revert back to it from time to time.

Tammy went around showing her ring because everyone was so excited to see it, one solitaire diamond that erupted out of a silver band. She answered the typical question of "how did he propose," by explaining everything in minute detail, since she was warned by these doting women not to leave anything out. After all the ooh's and aah's Maria served everyone a healthy portion of homemade chicken lasagna with a side of Caesar salad.

After the meal and everyone pitching in to clean up, they moved to the living room where they divided themselves amongst the two couches that were separated by a coffee table They washed their meal down with coffee and a tray that held a variety of cookies.

Tammy started the conversation with, "You guys I don't know where to begin. I'm super excited to be engaged because I love Jerome very much but I haven't known him for a long time. What if I don't really know him?"

"You still won't even if you've been together five years." They all laughed at Maria's comment.

"Craig and I got married after just two months." A couple women raised an eyebrow or tilted their head at Amanda. "And no, I wasn't pregnant." They all laughed again.

After she recovered from the unexpected comment and caught her breath, Laura added, "That's true. It doesn't matter how long you've been dating. But pray about it."

"And don't have sex with him until after you take your vows. It'll only muddy the waters and you won't see the truth; you'll only see what you want to see. You'll be blinded by the lust. You'll be one with him already so it'll be harder to see the flaws and the signs God is showing you," Janet warned.

"Amen," Maria held up a cookie in agreement.

"That's really hard. That's one reason we've been going out to eat a lot, so we won't be alone in either of our apartments."

"That's wisdom. Hold on to that," Amanda urged.

"We've come close a couple of times. And I don't trust myself. His body feels so good; his big arms and chest. God help me, please."

The room trickled with laughter.

"You better remember his body because it might not last long, Maria said. "We may have babies but their bodies change too."

"Huh, yes indeed."

"That's the truth."

"You can count on it." The confirmations came from all sides.

Tammy blushed. "Let me ask something else. Not that I think this but what if he's just putting on a facade? I've heard so many stories from the ladies at the hospital. Some of these men can be ruthless."

"It's good to see how he behaves with other people he knows, like his family and friends. Have you met any of them?" Laura waited for her answer as she took a sip of coffee.

"Yes, actually I've met his parents and his sister Barbara. They're really nice."

"That's good but have you asked them about him?"

"Yes, I've asked them how he was growing up?"

"No, not the surface questions. But really get with each of them individually and ask about what they feel are his bad qualities or habits; things you need to watch out for. You know stuff like that."

"Good point," Janet nodded her head.

"I'm not trying to make this feel like a wedding shower because he just proposed and you two have got a lot of time to get to know each other, but let's go around the room. Everyone give at least one piece of advice to Tammy, as she tries to get to know her fiancé better, and to make sure that he is who God has really chosen for her, her soulmate. I'll go first," Laura volunteered. She looked back at Tammy. "See if you can get him to tell you the worst obstacles he had to overcome when growing up. That will reveal a lot about the baggage he'll bring into your marriage and why he does what he does. He may overcompensate for some shortfall or he may inadvertently make you pay for something someone else did to him years ago."

Heads nodded as Tammy thought.

"Baby, you need to write this stuff down."

"I've already got it covered," Janet was frantically punching letters on her phone. "Her head is already in the clouds. She's not even thinking straight."

"O.K. Here's one. Make sure you ask him if he has any kids already, and what the circumstances are around the baby's momma. You definitely want to know how much he's obligated to pay in child support because that will be coming out of your household for a long time, even after they're eighteen. When you marry the man, you marry his kids too and if they ever want to come live with you, that's a sacrifice you need to make because a father deserves the right to parent his own child. And don't treat that child any differently than the children you actually birthed. Love them all. Now as far as their mother, I don't know what to tell you. God is still working on me with that. Because if you disrespect me, I'm gonna get with you."

"Alright, alright, we feel your pain," Janet tried to calm Amanda down. "My advice to you is to go to marriage counseling *before* you get married. You need to be upfront with each other about who you are and what you like and don't like and a counselor can bring out issues you didn't even know you had. This will give you a chance to talk through them and share your expectations before old habits develop."

"Si, es muy importante."

"Yes, I agree, that is very important. Premarital counseling is crucial. I can attest to that. This was eye opening for Frank and I."

Heads nodded.

"Tammy, my advice to you is to always remember why you fell in love with him in the first place. You'll need to fall back on that in bad times. And there will be plenty of them. You may not be able to imagine this but there will be times when you want to be as far from him as possible. Your husband can hurt you the most, believe me. He'll say things to you that will shake you to your core. There may be times when you doubt that God even brought you two together. In those times you'll need to stand on God's word. Keep the faith, and remember your marriage vows. Mija, society takes marriage lightly but it is a covenant between you and God and your husband. It's meant to be lasting, forever. Don't rush this process of getting to know each other. No, you won't know everything about him, but try and learn all you can. You already know about being unequally yoked, but that's not just about making sure you marry a Christian, it can include your background, values, what's important to you, if you want kids or not—"

"Indeed," Laura chimed in.

"What your goals are, attitudes about money—"

"Uggh, money, yes," Janet shook her head.

"You're taking two completely different people and combining them into one. It's not easy, no matter who you are," Maria concluded.

"Speaking of money, this win could help your marriage or hurt it, if you're not on the same page," Laura said.

"And don't think having it, will protect your marriage either," Janet warned.

"About that, everyone was pretty adamant about me getting a prenup, and I'm kind of nervous about asking him. I don't know how to even bring it up."

Let our attorney help you with that. He'll probably know how to approach it, especially from a man's perspective on being asked to sign one," Laura offered.

"Yeah, that can get touchy. And a man's ego is so fragile," Amanda put her cup and saucer down on the coffee table.

"See what the attorney says and then if you want to run it by us or the men, let us know." Maria gave Tammy's hand an encouraging pat. "No worries, Mija, it will work out."

With that, everyone sensed that their time was over. They gathered their cups and everything else and headed to the kitchen. After they persuaded Maria that it was easier to let each of them wash their own cup and saucer than for her to do them all herself, they all thanked her for the delicious meal, said their good-byes and gathered their belongings to leave.

"Thank you again. You all gave me a lot to think about," Tammy admitted. She walked to her car and sat there for a brief moment, making up in her mind that her next move was to call their attorney.

Chapter 21

Solo

TAMMY WASTED NO time getting an appointment with the lawyer. Since everyone in the lotto pool were uncompromising about making sure she got a prenup she felt it was the right thing to do. After parking her car into the parking garage she walked under the covered path into the lobby where she took the elevator to the third floor. After exiting she turned the handle of one of the double doors that opened into the law offices and greeted the secretary at the front desk. After the lady saw her name in the computer she acknowledged that Mr. Roberts would see her shortly and to please have a seat.

As Tammy walked toward the corner of the waiting area she walked past an open door and noticed what looked like rows and rows of brown books that seemed identical with their thick red and blue labels near the top and bottom of the spines as they stood erect on the book shelves. She took a seat and was soon greeted by their collective lawyer, Mr. Timothy Roberts.

Mr. Roberts was an average looking man who must have been in his fifties. Dressed in a simple but clearly expensive outfit of a light blue Rochester button down shirt and Ralph Lauren smoky-gray slacks that were set off with coal black Florsheim shoes. Tammy had to look up to him as she shook his hand and he led her to his office, which would be her first time seeing. The other times she had been at the firm were with everyone from the lottery pool and they had been ushered into a big conference room with a long table.

She now walked into Mr. Roberts's office which was about half the size of the conference room, and was still sizeable. His commanding desk and book shelf which were directly across from the entry immediately grabbed her attention and made her feel like she had just entered the chambers of a judge. With a matching round table that was big enough to fit in someone's kitchen on the left side of the office and a burgundy leather sofa that faced the large flat screen television on the right side. The furniture must have been purchased as one big set because the sofa matched the chairs that circled the table, all lined with bronze nail heads.

Tammy noticed the usual framed degrees on the wall but they were bordered by two other framed sayings, one titled The Lawyer's Creed on the left and The Lawyer's Prayer on the right. Mr. Roberts picked up a document from his desk and handed it to Tammy and motioned for her to take a seat in front of his desk. She looked at the heading and then looked back at him now seated behind his desk.

"When you called my secretary and told her you wanted to talk about a prenup, I took the liberty of drafting this up. And judging by the ring on your finger, I believe congratulations is in order."

"Oh, yes, thank you. Well, my friends think I should get one but I'm not really sure. I've always heard that if you really love someone, a prenup isn't necessary."

"You know who says that, broke people."

She chuckled.

"I've been at this for over thirty years and people with a lot of money, are always a target. People want to sue them, and marry them for all the wrong reasons and those who don't have what we call a prenuptial agreement are not protected. I advise all my wealthy clients to get one. I know you've seen these entertainers and actors lose half of their wealth when they got a divorce. And it doesn't matter whether they are male or female."

"But my fiancé doesn't even know I have money, no one knows."

"It doesn't matter, once you're married anything either of you own individually can be considered common property and split straight down the middle. The only way to protect yourself is with a prenup."

Tammy looked over the first page of the document, reading terms like "prospective husband" and "wish to establish their respective rights" and she began to feel knots in her stomach. Sensing her uneasiness Mr. Roberts tried to make her feel more comfortable with the idea.

"Tammy, you may be feeling like most women do, that this feels so formal and unromantic, that doing this seems to overshadow the love between you but if someone really loves you, they ultimately shouldn't have a problem signing this. There are many ways we can draft this. We can ensure the money always solely belongs to you or we can put a clause that states after so many years of marriage the money is joint property, however you feel comfortable. By the way, do you plan on telling him about the money?"

"Yes, but not until a few years after we're married. What do you suggest?"

"I can't give you any advice on if or when to tell your future husband but what I can do is give you some pro's and con's to consider while making your decision. And I can tell you a few stories of what happened with some of my clients. Some made it work and a few refused to go to the altar after they were asked to sign one. Let me say that most of my clients who initiate a prenup are men and they for the most part have no problem with the idea because they want to protect what they've worked so hard to accumulate. Women on the other hand, like yourself are more passive and usually doubt themselves, and go against their initial instinct, and sometimes the obvious, and they risk protecting what they've built or inherited due to their feelings of love."

"What do you mean by obvious?"

The lawyer looked at her for a second, contemplating how much to divulge. "Tammy, a lot of people I see, when they love someone, they get so caught up in being in love that they don't pay attention to the person they are in love with. They miss clues, and assume that just because someone says they love you, that they're the person they're supposed to spend the rest of their life with. I don't know anything about your fiancé but make sure you are careful to observe his behaviors not just what he says. Sometimes it's easier for an outsider to really see a person for who they are because the person who's actually in the relationship is too involved and too caught up in emotion to actually see the truth, or make wise decisions."

"Well, how would I...what excuse could I give for even having one drawn up?"

"To protect *you*. The draft you're holding is all inclusive. It covers your possessions, income, and assets pre-marriage. We also have ones that cover those same items that can be kept separate even if they are acquired during the marriage, but I didn't think you wanted that."

Tammy shook her head "no" in agreement.

Mr. Roberts pointed to the document. "This states that financial assets, and it explains that it covers income, inheritance, etc., are part of your estate pre-marriage and nowhere does it say anything about you having to disclose any of it."

Tammy looked at him.

"Now to answer your question specifically, I can explain to your fiancé that you were advised to protect your premarital assets in the event that he is incapacitated and cannot mentally or physically make decisions on his or your behalf. In the event that someone in his family, a selfish aunt or surprise love child, pops up and wants to claim some of his estate, anything you have before you two are married will be protected. If he's a stand up fellow and is with you for the right reasons, he'll see the logic in that and his first priority will be to protect you."

"And if not?"

"Then at least you know up front, who you're dealing with. And don't make excuses for him, however he reacts. I see that a lot as well with women. Trust what he will show you. And if you still make the decision to marry or not to marry, or stick to your guns and have him sign or surrender completely, own up to the choice you make. And remember it's much harder to get a spouse to sign a postnuptial than a prenuptial because after you're married they have no incentive; they've already got you.

"I understand. I'll do it. Let me read over this and see if I want to make any changes."

And with that Tammy stood, shook the attorney's hand and assured she'd get back to him before the week ended.

Chapter 22

Meeting of the Minds

ANOTHER SATURDAY MORNING had come and now it was approaching lunch time for Pastor David, which usually meant breaking bread with his co-laborers in the gospel, his pastor friends. Normally they would all meet at a nice and frugal restaurant, but Pastor David received a call the night before requesting they all meet for lunch at his church. Pastor David didn't think much of this request, since his church anniversary was coming up. He thought they might want to pray for him and his ministry inside the church building. This made perfect sense, being that they had done the very same thing once before. But, that was not there intention this time.

Pastor arrived to the church early enough to walk around to the side of the building and see the progress made on the youth center. He was so excited to be able to have the money needed to build it just the way he envisioned, without having to sacrifice on amenities due to lack of funds. Being the kind of pastor he was, he not only consulted the leaders and parents in the congregation, but also conducted a roundtable with all of the kids in the church to make sure he got their input on what they wanted and needed in a youth center.

When he followed up with the kids in the church about how their input would be executed, he was answered with cheers and hugs of appreciation. Just thinking about it kept a smile on his face. He walked back to the main building and to his car to retrieve the lunch he had bought for all of his colleagues and headed toward his office. After setting the food down, he went inside the sanctuary to pray.

Shortly after Pastor David got up from the altar, and had walked back to his office, his fellow pastors showed up. One by one, they all greeted each other and congratulated Pastor David on another year.

While eating lunch, they began to converse on how nice the new addition of the youth center was and what a blessing it would be not only to Pastor David's church, but to the entire community. Then the discussion took an unpleasant turn…

"Pastor, I would like to do something similar at my church, how did you do it?" Pastor Keith asked sincerely. Pastor Keith had only been pastoring for a few years, four if Pastor David remembered correctly, and his congregation was full of eager workers who wanted to make a difference in their poverty-stricken community.

"We've had a building fund for a few years, and that has had moderate success. Some years were very well and some not so good, but what really put us over the top was a donation," Pastor David said.

"Corporate?" Pastor Henry asked.

"I don't think so. I believe it was from a person."

"What do you mean; you weren't curious to know who it was?" Pastor Anthony asked.

"Well, they gave anonymously."

"Anonymously, what do you mean?" Pastor Keith asked.

"They didn't give their name," Pastor Henry defined.

"I know what it means," Pastor Keith chuckled, "but how did they do it? Did they just put a wad of money in the offering?"

"No, a cashier's check," Pastor David clarified.

"And you have no idea who could have done it?" Pastor Henry inquired.

"No, I really don't. And I'm not trying to figure it out. Look, the reason they used a cashier's check is so they didn't have to sign their own name so they clearly don't want anyone to know who they are," Pastor David answered.

They were assuming the donation was done at church, in an offering plate. He didn't mention that the donation was mailed in because he didn't want them drawing any conclusions from that piece of information. The less they knew, the better.

"Really...that's interesting," Pastor Anthony thought.

"You know, there's a rumor going around that someone in your church won the lottery," Pastor Henry informed.

"Really, why do they say that?" Pastor David leaned back in his chair.

"Because not too long ago, somebody got the winning numbers from that gas station right around the corner from here," Pastor Henry continued.

"Hmmm, OK. Well, who knows!" Pastor David shrugged his shoulders.

"Wait a minute, you're OK with that?" Pastor Anthony asked.

"Of course I am; why wouldn't I be?" David looked around to see if there was any surprise or concern on the other pastors' faces.

"If someone at my church wanted to give money they got by gambling, I wouldn't accept it," Pastor Anthony said emphatically.

"Why not," Pastor Henry asked before Pastor David had a chance to.

"And how would you even know?" Pastor Keith added.

"I'd ask them myself."

"You would actually do that?" Pastor Keith asked. "And what amount would you determine was big enough to ask?" he continued.

"Come on, Keith. You'll know the amount. Anything that looks unusual," Pastor Anthony said.

"But why wouldn't you accept it?" Pastor David asked the question again.

"Do you actually think God is going to bless someone by gambling?" Pastor Anthony asked. "He said tithes and offerings, *then* he'd pour out a blessing. All this gambling stuff is from the devil."

The room was silent. Pastor David looked at Pastor Anthony for a moment but didn't say anything. He wandered what his motive was. Pastor Anthony had been pastoring for many years, just as Pastor David, but Pastor Anthony's congregation was four times as big as his and he wandered if Pastor Anthony would still feel the same way if his congregation was smaller like it was when he first started.

He wasn't sure if the other pastors were reluctant to share their opinion because the size of their congregations are relatively small compared to Pastor Anthony's but that didn't matter to Pastor David. Just because your church is bigger doesn't make you more correct than a pastor who leads a small church.

Pastor David broke the silence. "The Bible doesn't say anything about accepting or not accepting tithes, offerings, or donations from the results of gambling. In this case, no one even knows how they got the money but it doesn't matter, and you can't just make the assumption that this money is bad because it might have come from it. The money that people give to our churches, none of us knows where it comes from. You don't know what everyone's occupation is. You might have money from drug dealers, prostitutes, a corrupt business man; you just don't know. And that's not my concern, that's God's. And it's not our job to ask. We pray over the money and ask God to give us direction on how to use it wisely. That's it."

Silence again.

Finally, Pastor Henry cleared his throat as if summoning up enough courage to somewhat contradict Pastor Anthony's refusal to accept gambling money, and added, "You know a lot of churches put an unnecessary yoke on the people because they put more restrictions on them than the Bible does, with their man-made rules. You'd make a good Pharisee." The room erupted with laughter with his lighthearted joke, yet Pastor Anthony's face remained unchanged.

"The Bible says that a fool chases fantasies," he countered.

"Yes, I know what Proverbs 12:11 says. That's a warning, not a commandment. People do what they want to do. I can't stop them from wasting their money at the casino or on a lottery ticket," Pastor David answered.

"Notice you said waste," Pastor Anthony quickly shot back.

"Right, I do feel that a lot of people, in my church and yours, all over the country for that matter, waste their money gambling. But you can waste your money in any way imaginable. My wife thinks I waste money on the cable bill every month but she knows that's what I like so we sacrifice and pay it. With gambling, there are some people who *are* addicted but there are other people who just do it for fun and that's all."

"Yeah, they have the right to spend their money on what they want to, as long as it's not hurting anybody," Pastor Keith added.

"But it is hurting people," Pastor Anthony pleaded, "It's like a tax on the poor. Most of the people who buy lottery tickets are poor people who can't afford it."

"But that's a choice they make. Nobody made them buy a ticket or go gamble their rent money," Pastor Henry noted.

"No, but the advertising targets the poor and uneducated," Pastor Anthony continued, "It lures them in with the false assumption of winning big but there's no way with those odds…"

"You stand a better chance getting struck by lightning twice than to win the lottery," Pastor Keith interrupted.

"That may be but again, some people just play for the fun of it," Pastor David said.

"Yeah, I'm thinking about renting a few vans and taking a church trip over to Coushatta," Pastor Keith said.

"Oh Lord, have mercy!" Pastor Anthony railed back in his chair throwing up his hands. "Brother, please don't do that. Don't make a mockery of the church."

"How is that a mockery? Do you know how many church members go to Coushatta, Vegas, even Branson, just to gamble? I don't see anything wrong with it," Pastor Keith continued.

"Wait, wasn't that your church's women's ministry that were asking for donations to buy raffle tickets for a chance to win a big screen T.V.?" Pastor Henry asked Pastor Anthony.

Pastor Anthony shot straight up in contempt. "I'd never condone something like that. That's just a church-sponsored lottery."

"Calm down brother," Pastor Keith pleaded with Pastor Anthony, motioning him to sit back down. Then, looking at Pastor Henry, Keith said, "It was my church, you want some tickets?" They both laughed.

"But seriously," Pastor Keith continued, "we've raised a lot of money with these 'lottery' fundraisers. We have baskets for Valentine's day that may include tickets to a comedy show; we've raffled off a weekend beach house getaway. We've done a lot of creative stuff that the members come up with. It gives people a chance to win an expensive gift they would probably never buy and the church gets blessed through the process as well."

"That's what's wrong with churches today, they're too intertwined with the world. You don't know where the world ends and the church door begins. The church has got to set some type of standard," Pastor Anthony preached.

"The church does set the standard, but a lot of people don't go to church now, because that standard is so high that you can't even enjoy life. The church's standard shouldn't be above God's standard. It should reflect God's standard. Now, don't get me wrong brother, the Bible doesn't spell out every single thing that you should and shouldn't do, it lays out principles and guides that we follow, and I don't see anywhere in the Bible where it's wrong," Pastor Keith said, defending his stance.

"Brothers, I think it would be best that we just agree to disagree, at this point," Pastor David concluded, trying to diffuse the discussion and Pastor Anthony's temper, "but I would like to briefly get your opinions on what you would do with the money. I've already made some decisions with the help of the church, as you can see outside with the youth center, but I just wanted to get a pastor's perspective."

"Well, I'd share the blessings. I'd pick a church that's worse off than yours and bless them financially. And if you take my advice on that, you don't have to search far, you can start with mine," Pastor Keith joked.

"It would be nice if you could bless some of your members. If there's a single mom who's catching the bus, it'd be nice to get her a car," Pastor Anthony said.

"I'm leaning more toward using the money to provide services like teaching life skills because if you just give people money without changing their behavior, they're going to blow it," Pastor Henry added.

Pastor Keith points out, "I have a lot of families where a couple thousand dollars could change their life."

"Really...you think it would *really* change lives? I've seen some of your members where the woman's wearing a two hundred dollar weave but her baby's hair is not even combed. They've got to make better decisions with what they already have," Pastor Henry commented. "And we have those type of women and men in my church too," he chuckled, "especially the men who sport the expensive rims that cost more than their car."

"O.K. brothers, I see you want to debate *and* laugh this morning. I appreciate your insight. I understand both sides. It's a lot to consider. I ask that you continue to pray for me as I try to be directed by The Holy Spirit. Thank you guys for coming out," Pastor David stood, signaling it was time to go.

"Let's pray for you and your ministry before we leave," Pastor Anthony said.

"Yes."

"Of course."

They all gathered around Pastor David, each touching him on the shoulder. Pastor Anthony started the prayer and each pastor afterward, as they prayed for his continued wisdom and understanding on how to use the donation. They also prayed for his congregation to respond in a positive and constructive way toward the decisions made regarding the money.

With that, each pastor gathered their belongings and left Pastor David's office, showing themselves out of the church building, as he walked back to the altar to seek God's face once more.

Chapter 23

The Test

THE SUN'S RAYS shining through the blinds like piercing white light, danced on her eyelids, finally waking Laura up. She turned to see what time it was. The clock showed 9:00 am. She made up her mind that this was going to be a laid-back Saturday. She was going to relax and read and watch movies. She heard noises coming from Frank's tablet from what sounded like the kitchen. He always beat her getting up. After going through her morning ritual she headed for the kitchen but bee-lined it back to the bedroom when she realized she didn't have her cell phone. After unplugging it from the charger she went back toward the kitchen to eat.

"Good morning," Laura headed straight for the refrigerator and took out the mason jar that held her overnight oats, she had prepared the night before. She got a spoon out of the drawer and sat at the table with Frank who was already pouring a second bowl of cereal.

"What do you have going for the day?" Frank's eyes toggled from her to his screen.

"Absolutely nothing, I'm just going to relax," Laura unscrewed the top and scooped up the mixture of bananas, strawberries, and yogurt, on top and layered between the oatmeal and milk blend."

"I've got a few errands to run then I'll be back." Frank shoveled another spoon in his mouth and turned his attention back to his tablet.

Laura touched the screen of her cell and started catching up on what she'd missed. She quickly scanned the home screen; a couple of text messages, ten Facebook notifications, and one missed call. "Oh, my mom called, I didn't hear it." She searched for the time she'd called and noted that it was earlier that morning. *Eight o'clock on a Saturday. That's unusual.* She would call her mom back after she finished eating.

Laura got half way through the creamy concoction when her phone rang. It was her mom again. She hadn't left a voicemail earlier but to call her twice in approximately two hours and before ten a.m. on a Saturday; something was wrong.

"Mamma, you O.K.?"

"Hi Laura, yes baby, I'm fine. I just want to see what you thought about something."

"What's wrong?" she could hear it in her mom's voice.

"Well, Maury called here early this morning upset because they repossessed his car and he asked if he could borrow some money to get another one."

Laura slammed her hand on the table before she knew it. "You've got to be kidding. What does that have to do with you?"

"Well we could help him out, I mean we have this money—"

"And he knows that, that's why he's asking, Mamma. What did Daddy say?"

"I can't get him on the phone. He's down there at the barber shop so he either left his phone in the car or he's got it on silent or something. You know he's not good with working that phone."

"Mamma, do not give Maury any money," Laura jerked up from the table and stomped to their bedroom. "You know you're not gonna get that money back."

"You're probably right, but how can I see my son in need and not give it to him when we have it to give?"

"Because he's a grown man and he shouldn't be asking his parents for anything."

"Maybe the Lord blessed us with this money right on time because he knew this was going to happen."

Lord give me strength. "No, this blessing is for you and Daddy, not Maury."

"Well Laura, it's not like he isn't trying, he's just run into some hard times."

"Mamma, he doesn't have any kids, no responsibilities, he should have some money somewhere."

"Laura, you know he lost his job that time—"

"That was over a year ago. And he should have recovered by now. Besides that's what unemployment is for. And you don't know if he did something wrong to lose his job. Knowing Maury he was probably showing up late and they got tired of it." Laura had to calm herself down, the last thing she wanted to do was upset her mother so she lowered her voice. "Mamma, Maury is irresponsible and he's going to keep on doing stuff like this if you keep coming to his rescue."

"But if we could pay for him a car, outright, he wouldn't have to worry about a car note and that could really help him get some traction."

"Mamma, I'm telling you whatever you do, it still won't be enough. He'll come up with something else next month. That money was for y'all and you're going to wind up giving most of it to him and I promise you, he's going to wind right back up in the same situation. Mamma, I'm telling you don't do it, at least talk to Daddy first." Laura couldn't take it anymore. "Mamma, I've got to call you back."

"You're not going to call Maury are you?"

"Yes, I am," Laura separated her words for emphasis.

"No, Laura, this is just between us."

"I'm sorry Mamma, I'm not gonna sit here and let him swindle you. I'll talk to you later. Sorry, bye." She was careful not to have her mom think she was hanging up in her face. Without missing a beat, Laura switched her focus on what she would say to her brother.

Laura pushed the button to call Maury. It rang three times then went to voicemail. *He sent me to voicemail.* She gritted her teeth and called him again. This time it went straight to voicemail. She threw her phone down and walked to her closet, looking for some clothes to change into. She was not about to sit around and let Maury do this to her parents. She didn't give that money for him to just nickel and dime it all away from them. This was too much. She had to do something. She didn't know what but she had to get to her parents' house.

Frank heard the commotion she was making and came into the bedroom. "What happened?"

Laura gave him the details and he shook his head. He already knew what she was about to do. "I

164

know you're upset but you have got to calm down before you get behind the wheel."

She looked at him and breathed in a long slow breath but her face was still stonewalled. She tied her tennis shoes and grabbed her phone. "I don't know when I'll be back," She charged past him and snatched her keys off of the counter, leaving without another word.

No sooner had she hopped in her car and closed the driver's side door that she figured she would try her dad. He picked up.

"Hel—"

"Daddy, have you talked to Mamma?"

"No, what's wrong?"

"She's been trying to call you. Maury's car got repossessed and he's trying to convince her to buy him a new one."

"What?"

"Did Maury call you?"

"No, I haven't talked to him. This is the first I've heard of this. Let me call your mother. And I'm about to go home, I'll be there shortly."

"Me too, I'm coming over."

"That's not necessary, just sit tight. Let me see what's going on. I'll call you back."

"O.K." is all she could muster. She wanted to object but knew he needed to get off of the phone with her and talk to Mamma. Laura felt helpless. She couldn't call her mom back or try Maury again because her dad could be trying to get in touch with both of them. So she just sat there with the car running, wondering what she should do next. She called Frank.

"Frank."

"What happened?"

"I don't know yet. You want to go with me?"

"Where?"

"To my parent's house."

"Aren't you—"

"I haven't left yet, I'm still in the driveway."

"What do you expect me to do?"

"Help me talk some sense into my parents."

"What, your dad is going along with this foolishness?"

"He didn't know about it. He's supposed to be calling my mom and he's on his way home." She left out the fact that her dad wanted her to wait until he called back. If Frank knew that, he wouldn't go.

"Look, I'll go but I'm not going to offer any advice. If they ask me what I think, then I'll say something."

"O.K."

"And, if Maury is over there, I'm not saying anything to him about it either."

"But, I need you to talk to him man to man and let him know what he's doing is foul."

"If your dad can't convince him, he's not going to listen to me. And besides, your parents may have an issue with me saying anything to their son."

"You know they love you just like you were their own son."

"Yeah, but if Maury starts loud talking me and I do the same to him, they're going to be on his side no matter if he's wrong or not. It's just like breaking up a fight between a couple; even if the woman is getting beat up by the man, if you get him off of her and threaten to hit him, she'll start hitting you. So I'm telling you now, I'm not going to interfere in a family situation."

"O.K. I get it."

"Hold on, I'll be right there."

Several minutes passed and Frank was in the car, which made Laura feel better since now she didn't feel like she was alone, like it was her against the world, well her family.

"Does Nell know about this?"

"I don't know but she won't hear it from me. She doesn't care. If anything, if she knows that Maury is benefiting from anything, she'll think she's entitled to some money too." Laura called the house again but there was no answer and there was no sense in trying to get Maury; he was busy scheming.

They finally arrived at her parent's house and Laura pulled into the driveway, Frank refusing to drive because if they saw them pull up he didn't want anyone thinking that it was his idea to come. Laura took out the key she has had since childhood, unlocked the door, while simultaneously ringing the doorbell one time and rushed inside leaving Frank about five strides behind her.

She called out her parents' names but got no response. She found her mother in her bedroom as Frank waited in the living room. After a few minutes, they both came out and joined Frank. Maggy only stayed long enough to give Frank a hug then headed for the kitchen. They followed, but not before Laura whispered to Frank that her father was with Maury.

Both of them stood in the kitchen watching. Laura didn't want to jump in asking a bunch of questions because she was more calm now, since her mom had told her that her dad was actually with Maura. She was sure he would talk some sense into him. Since the coast was clear, Frank asked if he could go watch T.V. in the den while Laura helped her mom in the kitchen.

After Frank left the room, they talked a bit. Maggy didn't offer up any more information so Laura didn't ask, she was sure to get the rundown from her father when he got back. And there was no need to make her mom feel bad or press her point about the same things she had earlier during their phone call. There was no need to convince her mom, when her dad would do it anyway. For now, Laura was just content to spend some time with her and was relieved her dad was handling Maury.

A couple of hours had passed and Laura fought the urge to call her dad, she didn't want to interrupt anything he was telling Maury. She could imagine her dad scolding Maury for his irresponsibility and carelessness. Hopefully her brother would get his act together after this talk. She was just about to ask Frank if he was ready to leave when she heard the short beep from the house alarm system and the front door open.

Daddy stepped into the room looking worn out and Maury was right behind him, his eyes dancing. Laura stood and hugged her father but didn't even say hello to her brother, she was too busy wondering why he looked so happy.

"Hey Sis."

"Maury," her voice ringing with doubt.

"What's up brother-in-law?"

"Hey, Maury."

He then kissed their mom on the cheek and gave her an unusually long hug. "Thanks again, Mamma."

"O.K. Maury." Their mom's voice was uneasy.

"Well, I'll see you all later. I've got to get home and get ready for work in the morning. I'll be working all the overtime I can. See you Sis, Frank." Then he proceeded to the doorway and Laura was waiting for their father to get up too, to take Maury back home but he didn't move. It was then that Laura's brain registered the faint noise of keys clanging together.

168

Daddy was actually loaning Maury his car. She didn't know if that was a good idea or not.

Frank spoke up. "So you stopped sporting your big Mercedes emblem?" referring to the over-sized key ring Maury normally had with him.

"Those are Daddy's keys," Laura turned to Frank.

"No, they're not my keys," Tom looked at his wife in disappointment so Laura focused on her mom as well. Maggy looked down, refusing to make eye contact with either one of them.

Laura looked at Maury. "What's going on?"

He smiled from the corner of his mouth then addressed Frank. "I've got a new ride. Wanna see it?"

"What do you mean?" Laura's pulse began to rise and she stole a glance at everyone in the room, wanting someone, anyone to explain what was going on.

"Yes," Frank hesitated. Laura's question was ignored. Frank followed Maury to the front door and Laura got up as well, looking at her parents again, her brow wrinkled seeking answers. They remained silent.

When Laura got outside she almost choked on her own saliva and had to breathe in a quick puff of air. She could not believe her eyes.

A black Cadillac Escalade sat in the driveway. Maury pushed a button to start it up. "Maury this is yours?" Frank asked the rhetorical question. "Chrome alloy wheels, nice."

"Thanks." Maury opened the door wider to show the leather interior and pushed a button to open the sunroof. He then reached to cut on the stereo to demonstrate the state-of-the-art Bose speakers to Frank. Noise filled the street and Laura had seen enough. "How did this happen?" She stared directly at Maury.

"What do you mean?"

"Maury, don't play games with me. How did you get this?"

"Mamma bought it for me."

"How could you?"

"Laura, my car got repossessed and I asked Mamma if she would help me get something else."

"And Daddy went along with this?"

"It was already taken care of before he got home. I just took him on a joy ride. He was a little upset but we talked and I explained myself—"

"You took advantage of our mother! You knew I was calling you but you wouldn't even pick up the phone. How can you be so selfish? Every time I look up, you're asking them to bail you out of something. You're a grown man, Maury. When are you going to take responsibility and stop leeching off of our parents?"

He turned his attention to his brother-in-law hoping he would understand. "Man, Frank, my car was upside down, the interest was too high, I just couldn't afford the payments anymore."

"I don't know man," Frank motioned to the vehicle, "this is a bit much. Why this?"

"I still have to be presentable."

Laura came unglued. "Presentable? Are you kidding? This is luxury, and you can't afford luxury so you get a cash car. You could have gotten a car for less than two thousand dollars." Laura lowered her voice, "Mamma just got that money and she can't even enjoy it because she spent a lot of it on you. You swindled her. You couldn't wait to come up with some excuse to get your hands on her money."

"Laura, she could have said no but she wanted to help. I don't see anything wrong with that."

Laura wanted to punch her brother in the face. Her demeanor gave her away and Frank leaped in between them, holding Laura back by the waist.

Maury shook his head. "So that's how it is, Laura? O.K. I got you." He pushed up on the runner and hopped into his new vehicle. "Bye, Frank." And after grimacing toward his sister, he rolled the window up and drove off. She could hear the music of his system even with the windows up, and as the distance grew between them she could still hear the bass pounding in the air.

"Frank, what do I do?" she turned to face him. He blinked; his mouth wide open. He could only offer shrugged shoulders. They both headed back inside.

Laura, clearly shaken, plopped on the couch and searched her parents' eyes for answers.

"Laura I know you're upset, but I would've done it for any of my kids."

"You shouldn't have to. And Frank and I would never ask you to do something like this. I didn't give—," she almost slipped, "expect you to give your money to any of us."

"Daddy, why didn't you do something?"

Tom shook his head. "Everything was already done before I got home. Your mom had signed the papers and everything."

"How? Mamma, you bought a forty thousand dollar car for him? You blew a lot of the money you just got. That was for you and daddy and neither one of us have the right to ask you for it."

"Laura, it's not as bad as you think."

"I didn't pay for the whole thing. I almost did but they had a zero percent interest for eighteen months and they knocked six thousand off the price

171

so I just co-signed the loan. It's in Maury's name though. That way he can build his credit back up."

"Build his credit back up? Mamma, Maury's not gonna act right. And why didn't you wait on Daddy?"

"Well, I did get on Maury about that. He did kind of put me in an awkward position."

"He drove the Escalade to the house with the salesman and handed your mamma the paperwork with everything drawn up. So he's got a stranger in my house shoving papers and a pen in my wife's face."

"What the…" Laura's wide eyes stared at her dad. She couldn't believe it. "How did he even get to the dealership?

"He rode the Metro bus," Tom folded his arms.

Frank dropped his head, and pinched the stem of his nose, like he was trying to hold back a headache.

"Mamma, do you not see what's going on? Maury orchestrated this whole thing. Why do you think he called you instead of Daddy?"

"He couldn't reach your Daddy."

"O.K. Fine." Laura tried another approach. "Mamma, why didn't you just say, 'No?'"

"He needs a car to get back and forth to work."

"Didn't he just catch the bus to go to the dealership? Why can't he catch the bus to work?"

"The lines don't run to his job."

"Then Uber or a taxi."

"That's not reliable. You've got to call every day. And a taxi is expensive." Maggy defended.

"Mamma, when are you going to stop making excuses for him? He's a grown man. You keep bailing him out. He's never going to learn. You've got to let him face the consequences of his bad choices." Turning to Tom, "Daddy if he just got a repossession that means he didn't pay. So how do you think he's gonna be able to pay for this one? He's not, watch and see. He may pay for a few months but it's not going to last. Nothing ever does with Maury because he knows that anytime he messes up, he can come right back to his parents and you'll make it all better. You keep taking on his problems and trying to figure out a way to make things work when he won't even do it for himself."

"Laura, Maury is going to do right because I told him he better not mess up my name."

"Mamma, Maury doesn't even regard his own name. Do you actually think he has any respect for your name when he has no respect for his own? His car just got repossessed!" Frank squeezed Laura's leg in an attempt to get her to calm down. "Why do you think he needed you? He couldn't get something else on his own. The bank even had enough sense not to put his name on a forty thousand dollar SUV, that's why he came to you. They pulled his credit report and saw that he wasn't paying his bills on time and *they* have more money than you do, Mamma. And they still wouldn't take the risk." Laura sounded like she was scolding her mother but she had to get the point across. "And if you wanted to help Maury out, you should have gotten him a cash car. They have plenty of cars out there for less than two thousand dollars. It doesn't matter how it looks, just as long as it runs good, just enough to get him from point A to point B. Maybe then he would appreciate something. He needs to be humbled anyway."

"Laura, I understand what you're trying—"

"No, I'm sick of this," she cut her father off. "Y'all are gonna go to your grave still worrying about him. And he's just trying to get all he can get. You finally get a come up and you let him squander it away on a car. I'm done. Come on Frank, I've got to go."

And with that, Laura leaped from the couch and raced to the door.

Chapter 24

Tammy's Doubts

SHE COULD NOT sleep. Tammy lay in her bed all night, thinking and yes worrying, even though she knew what she was supposed to do instead, cast all her cares on The Lord. She really tried but she was so concerned about if she was doing the right thing. She was so sure that giving Jerome a prenup was the responsible thing to do. She had even talked to the men in the lottery pool soon after her second appointment with the lawyer, getting all the details down. And not only did their lawyer give her counsel by sharing situations he's seen with his clients, on both the female and male sides of the prenup dilemma, he also explained the negative consequences of a postnuptial, which she didn't even want to consider.

All the men were still in favor of her getting the prenup but what they all had in common was they were *already* married. They were only talking by what they think they would do or how they think they would respond, but they didn't actually have to walk in Jerome's shoes so she had to take their advice and the women's with a grain of salt. She had prayed about it but wasn't sure if God had given her an answer on the matter. He seemed silent, hence her tossing and turning all night.

How would Jerome take this? She thought about that for herself as well. She knew that if the roles were reversed, she would question why he would want a prenup. *What is he hiding,* she would sure be thinking. *He really doesn't trust me. He thinks I want his money.* Many thoughts invaded her mind.

Jerome had already told her that they could get married tomorrow as far as he was concerned but that he knew women liked to plan things out and that he'd be O.K. with whatever date she decided on. She couldn't even think about a wedding right now. There was too much they would have to go through before she would be ready to send out save-the-date invitations.

It had been a couple months since his proposal but she didn't want to set a date until she was sure he still wanted to go through with it after she dropped the prenup bomb on him. If she decided to go through with any type of agreement, she certainly knew it would have to be before marriage, not after.

But the question still remained, IF. If she was to push through her anxiety of what he might think, how he might feel, or what he might do in response, how would she even start the conversation? That's not a common topic to just toss into a discussion. And what if he totally freaked out and told his parents or his sister Barbara? What would they think of her? All of them seemed nice and she really thought her and Barbara could become close, but that was doubtful if she had any reservations as to why her soon to be sister-in-law was demanding her brother sign a contract.

And what would Jerome's parents think? She's sure he would tell them too. Would their smiles and warm wishes turn into disdain for their soon-to-be daughter-in-law? Would Jerome's mother take away her invitation to call her mom because she no longer trusted Tammy loves her only son?

The pressure was too much. Her mind and emotions were in overdrive, conjuring up scenarios that weren't logical. Or were they? Could soon-to-be family all of a sudden turn on you because of what you feel you need to do to protect yourself? And if they did, what did that say about them? Would they be a fair-weather family; only loving when things were going according to how they thought they should? If they turned on Tammy, would that be a warning to her that they would try to get in her and Jerome's business after they were married? *If they do it before marriage, it will only continue or get worse after marriage,* Tammy remembered her mother always warning her. The warnings were actually about men, more specifically, husbands-to-be but it applied to their families as well. If they are controlling before, they'll be more so after.

And if Jerome turned to his family for every issue they would face as a couple, what did that say about him or their relationship? They alone needed to think this through and decide how to handle this prenup. Maybe he wouldn't agree to all the stipulations and they'd have to revise the contract. Tammy was flexible but she would prefer for him to just sign it so they can get on with planning their wedding and life together. She might be totally overreacting. Maybe he loved her so much that he trusted her explicitly. She hoped that he didn't care what words were on the paper because he trusted her beyond his head, and with his heart.

She didn't know if that was realistic or not, since she ultimately didn't know what she would do if the situation were reversed. She just didn't know. Tammy suppressed the single tear welling up inside her. This was not what she wanted to be thinking about right now. This was supposed to be a time of pure happiness and anticipation; good anticipation over what lied ahead. She was tired of devoting so much time to these negative thoughts, all because she wanted, or was expected to be wise and protect her winnings, from even the man she loved.

Chapter 25

Don's Fight

GETTING READY FOR bed, Don sat on the side of their Jacuzzi tub and watched Janet brush her teeth. She's so into her routine that she doesn't even acknowledge him. She's deliberately not making any eye contact, acting like he's not even there. He felt invisible, a bystander on the outside looking in. He wanted to say something, but lately anything they talked about turned into an argument. He didn't know how his marriage had gotten to this state and he wanted to save it but Janet had already made it clear that she was done. She had flat out told him that winning the lottery money had made it easier for her to make the decision to leave him. He thought about what would have happened if they had never won. Janet's decision to give up on their marriage came soon after the win and that made him question a lot of things. Would she be trying harder if she didn't already have an easy way out financially?

Did she really still love him? Was she blowing this affection thing way out of proportion and using it as an excuse just to take her half of the money and leave? She had complained a few times before, but it had been years ago and he thought she had gotten over it. She hadn't brought it up again for so long, after all and he thought he was doing better.

Now here he was staring at his wife going through the mechanics of mouthwash, contacts, putting the floss away…never trying to engage him in any conversation while she brushed her hair, clearly avoiding eye contact with him. He had to say something. Maybe he would start out with an apology.

"Janet."

She slowly veered her eyes in his direction, looking through the bathroom mirror, never turning around.

"I wanted to explain to you that I was never taught how to love. I didn't know you needed all that touchy feely stuff. I wasn't focused on that. I was taught to be the provider and take care of my wife and kids and that's what I did."

"I don't want to hear your excuses. You weren't taught how to have sex either but you figured that out. As a matter of fact, you perfected that because it benefits you."

"You don't enjoy it?"

"Yes, but sex for women is more than just the bedroom, that's only about ten percent of it. The majority of it is supposed to happen outside the bedroom."

Don was dumbfounded but before he could respond, she added, "And don't act like you did all of this on your own, I worked too. I provide just as much income to this household as you do."

"I didn't mean it like that. What I'm saying is, no matter what happens I'm still responsible for providing for you and the kids."

Janet took it all in. She was tired of his explanations. They meant nothing anymore. She had given him the benefit of the doubt earlier in their marriage but she had also told him what she needed. And after that, she expected him to fulfill those needs, but it didn't happen. Anytime she complained, he would do better, but inevitably go back to his old ways of a nonchalant attitude. They had been down this road many times before.

Why does he want me to stay with him? She asked herself the question but needed an answer from him. She wanted to know his motives. *Does he want me or the money?* She looked him in the eyes hoping to see into his heart, but he had a question of his own.

"Do you value the money over our marriage?"

Janet's mouth dropped at the audacity of the question. "I'm a simple woman. I just want to be loved, that's it. Since you won't take the time to do that, I'd rather be by myself."

"You used to not be this way."

"And what way is that? You mean I used to not stand up for myself; I used to just accept whatever you were willing to give? Well, I'm tired, I'm just tired."

"So you come to this revelation after we win ten million dollars, how convenient."

"So you're just concerned about the money. You should be more concerned that your wife wants a divorce, but the only thing you can think about is material stuff!"

"I could say the same for you. You're so eager to take the money and run and throw away over twenty years of marriage."

"What good is a marriage if I'm miserable? This is not working. And when have you ever known me to be impressed with material things? You're the one who's always focused on status symbols. I didn't want that Mercedes but you were too busy worrying about what other people would think of *you*, that you disregarded what *I* wanted."

"I just wanted the best for you."

"But it's always on your terms." Janet stormed out of the bathroom. She got in bed and rolled over, clenching the covers around her body, while Don was reduced to another night on the floor.

***

Don walked into the counselor's office alone. He was embarrassed when he confirmed the appointment with the secretary the day before, having to mention that the session would be for him only since his wife refused to go. Now that he was here he was angry all over again to even be in this position, needing to see a counselor at all, and upset by the fact that he didn't have enough influence with his wife to get her to keep coming.

"Don, nice to see you again. Please have a seat."

Don dove right in. "I don't know what to do. She still wants to leave."

"Alright, let's start at the beginning. What signs did you miss or ignore?"

"Nothing—"

"No, this doesn't just come out of the blue. There were clues, what were they? Think back. What were her complaints, besides the ones she stated in here? And how did you address them?"

Don looked down.

"Don, I can see you're angry, but that will not solve anything. Use your anger constructively to find a solution. You've got to take some responsibility here. A woman needs to be heard, feel special, treated like a queen, because that's what they are. And when you do that, she will treat you like the king you are. You've got to really listen. From what I heard from her, you keep disappointing her. And she's given up."

"There's some truth to that, but I feel disrespected."

"How does she not respect you?"

"She questions me about money."

"It sounds like she doesn't trust your judgment, why is that?"

"Because one investment I made went bad."

"Tell me more about that."

Don recalled the time in their marriage when he got an investment tip about a company stock and bought in heavily. Things were good for years but when damaging information got out about the company, the stock plummeted and because of the type of portfolio he owned, he couldn't get out until the stock market closed at the end of the day, by that time it was too late. The stock wasn't worth anything. And their finances and marriage had taken a terrible blow.

"It sounds like you're trying to hit it big and make more money but that's not her priority. She wants security. You're blessed to have a wife that wants you and not your money. Your net worth doesn't determine your self-worth. You're more than your money." Don grunted at the irony of his statement. If he only knew how much money was at stake now.

Dr. Collins had a unique ability to see right at the heart of his clients. He sometimes couldn't tell them up front, because they wouldn't receive it; so he would guide them to discover it for themselves, adjusting his style based on the needs of the client. Sometimes he had hard-hearted clients like now and Don needed in-your-face, direct and confrontational coaching from him.

"Don, let me cut to the chase. The very thing you want, you're unwilling to give to your wife. She wants respect too but in a different way. Respecting her is not dismissing what she tells you is important to her. If you want to touch her heart, love her."

"I don't feel like she appreciates what I do for her."

"Don, you've got to put her first no matter what. You love her and you will experience the appreciation and respect you seek. It all falls on the man. That's just the way it is, because God holds you accountable for her. You need to put her needs first like Christ did us or you'll just keep going through the same cycle. Think about it. Christ died first before we even accepted him as savior so you need to do the same. I see a lot of men come in here and they say they'd die for their wives, yet they won't even fight for their wives, won't make sacrifices, won't suffer. Yes, I said suffer. It doesn't matter if you're the only one making the effort, and I don't believe that's the case here at all but if you really want her, fight for her. I'm not saying it's going to be easy. Don't expect much at the beginning. It may actually get worse before it gets better, but keep going.

Don's voice cracked, "I can't lose my wife."

"Do the things you did at first to get her. Chase after her again. If you won her over once, you can get her again. But it might be harder because you've got to press through all of the scar tissue around her heart, and you put it there, so she's not going to be receptive at first. She's now at the point where she doesn't care what happens to your marriage. In her mind, she's done but don't lose hope. Little by little you will see her walls come down and she will let you in again. God is on your side, because he hates divorce. Keep praying and asking God to soften her heart and feel love for you again. And you need to ask Him how to reach your wife and restore your marriage. Have faith, it can be done."

Don sat back, focusing his thoughts. The words "fight for her" stirred something up in his spirit and gave him hope. If he could fight for all the deals he's gotten over the years, fight past the no's, and even fight through financial blows, surely he could fight for the woman he fell in love with, the mother of his two grown children. He got up with a renewed determination to do whatever he could to get his wife back.

Chapter 26

Laura's Struggle

MONDAY MORNING COULDN'T get there fast enough. Laura was already dialing the lawyer's office at 8:01 a.m., trying to find a way around what happened over the weekend. She had to find a way to undo what her brother had done. She told the secretary it was urgent and she put the call through to Mr. Roberts.

"Hi Laura. I don't think I understood fully. Our secretary said something about your brother having made your parents buy him a car?"

"He made my mom co-sign for a Cadillac Escalade. Well, he didn't make her, he tricked her into doing it. Anyway, is there anything I can do?"

"It depends on what you mean by tricked."

"OK, not tricked, pressured."

"Explain exactly what happened." After Laura gave the details he gave some advice.

"Hmmm. Have they changed their mind and want to get rid of it or are you hoping to change their mind?"

"I'm hoping they'll change their mind."

"When did they buy it?"

"Saturday."

186

"If they want to give it back and have the chance to get all their money back I suggest getting the vehicle back to the dealer within three days. This is a long shot because you'll have to convince your parents and the dealership because there's no law requiring the business to take it back."

"And what if I can't do that? My mom believes everything my brother tells her and my dad just goes along with whatever my mom decides."

"They can always sell it later if they decide to but they'll be losing anywhere from fifteen to twenty-five percent of what the car is worth."

"Right."

"But let me tell you, even if you succeed, it may bring a wedge between not only you and your brother, but your parents as well."

"How is that, I'm just looking out for them."

"It doesn't matter. They may not see it that way. They may focus on the fact that you're interfering with what they want to do, whether it's bad for them or not. You need to think about how this is going to affect your relationship with them. Can you imagine what family gatherings will be like with all of that tension in the air? I know your heart is in the right place by trying to protect them but you may be fighting a losing battle."

"That money was for them. They were finally going to be able to do things they've wanted to do since I was a child."

"Look, you did an honorable thing. But when you give someone money as a gift, you've got to accept what they decide to do with it."

"No, I could have put terms in the acceptance of the money."

"Contingencies in certain situations may work but—"

Laura's mind was in overdrive. "I could have stipulated that it must be spent on them alone. Would that have worked?"

"That actually might have raised red flags for them. Laura, listen to me. I think the best thing you can do is let it go. Talk to your husband about it and see what he thinks but you're trying to change something that already happened and apparently against their will because they didn't have to do all this in the first place. You're letting this stress you out."

Laura let out a long sigh and sunk into her office chair. *Am I really going overboard with this?* She stared at the wall.

"Let me know if you need anything else but I need to go, I have another client waiting."

"Right, of course. Thank you for your time."

"You're welcome."

After the conversation, Laura thought about how her level of concern had skyrocketed once she had given her parents the money. She realized she wasn't fully enjoying these moments with her husband because she was too busy worrying about what her parents would do with their gift. All she wanted to do was bless them and give them the opportunities they never had before, and protecting them from anyone who threatened to jeopardize that, including her brother, was her responsibility. But she was starting to realize you can't protect someone who doesn't want to be protected, even if it's your own parents. She closed her eyes but could not shut back the tears that burst through the crevices, like water seeping through cracks in a dam.

Chapter 27

Prenup Reveal

THIS WAS IT. No more sleepless nights and no more wondering about what he might do or say. Tammy was going to present Jerome with the prenup. While they talked the night before, she casually told him there was something she needed to discuss and asked if he would come over that day. She waited to call him until she knew where to meet him. It took a moment to make up her mind. She thought about asking him to meet her in the office with the lawyer, but when she asked the guys' opinion, Craig in particular asked her if she was crazy. He said that would be totally disrespectful to spring that on Jerome in front of a total stranger. Frank had concurred and told her that would be a hard one for any man to get over. Tammy thought that would have been the most efficient thing to do so Jerome could ask the lawyer any questions right then and there and Mr. Roberts could also help her if she stammered over anything or didn't fully explain herself. They could have alternatively met in the conference room first and then asked the lawyer to join them afterward;

but she concluded that the men were right, and she abandoned the idea. But Tammy had asked for a walk-in appointment for the day just in case Jerome did want to talk to him.

After some guidance from the men, and after almost begging Mr. Roberts to coach her on what to say and what to absolutely avoid, Tammy now felt she was ready to do it.

She even persuaded the men to role play with her, but when Frank, playing like he was Jerome, started hollering at her and said the wedding was off, she was thrust into shock. And when he followed it up with asking for the ring back, she almost choked on her own tears. He was too believable, but they all insisted that she had to be ready for anything and if she could take the worst of what Frank's role play brought forth, she could face the unknown.

Their main concern was for Tammy to be sure of what she wanted to do and why she wanted to do it. If she knew those two things, she would be able to withstand any pressure that might come from Jerome or his family. And they wanted to be sure she was doing the right thing, not for any of them in the pool, but for herself. Tammy understood that now. And she was ready to get this behind them, whatever the outcome.

Tammy moved the contract to the corner table that separated the couches. Even though it was still in the envelope, she didn't want it to be in Jerome's immediate line of sight. She wanted to set the tone for the conversation and didn't want him to be taken aback by anything. She wondered if having a pen right there would be too much pressure for him so she decided against it.

She had spent more time than usual, thinking about what to wear for this meeting. This was not a date, they both were clearly aware of that. Even though he had no idea what she wanted to talk about this was indeed a meeting nonetheless and she wanted to dress appropriately. Not too professional but not too casual either. *What on Earth do you wear when you're handing your fiancé a contract that basically says even though I love you, I don't really trust you enough to let me keep all the money that I won before I met you?* She settled on a soft pink long sleeve cotton blend and khaki slacks with loafers.

Tammy's doorbell rung twice. *This is it,* she thought, *be strong and be understanding.* She opened the door and smiled but his appearance quickly turned her smile into a million butterflies playing around in her stomach. She wasn't sure if it was simply how attractive he was to her or any nervousness that she had desperately tried to pray away.

From his attire, it seemed he had the impression that she may have been having second thoughts about marrying him and he chose an outfit that would change her mind. Not that she was vain by any stretch of the imagination, but she was a woman and she did have eyes. He was wearing a white linen top that gripped every muscle in his chest. Or were her eyes seeing what they wanted to see? And his sand-colored pants could not mask the bulkiness of his quadriceps. *Focus,* she told herself. She didn't even want to get too close to him so she motioned for him to come in. *Get yourself together,* her mind pleaded as she locked the front door.

"No kiss?" Jerome's voice broke the silence.

"I'd really like to go over what I wanted to talk to you about first."

"Is everything alright? You're not getting cold feet on me are you?"

"No, not at all. And I hope, after this, you won't either."

"What's wrong?"

"I do love you, very much. And I do want to spend the rest of my life with you."

"But—"

"What would be the worst thing I could tell you right now?" She hoped what she was actually going to share wouldn't be nearly as bad as what his mind would conceive. She waited.

His demeanor turned serious. "That you cheated on me."

"No, never, not at all," the thought of such bruised her heart.

"I can take anything else, so just come out and tell me."

"I've been advised to get a prenup," she carefully watched him, never letting go of his gaze.

"A prenup?" his response let her know that not only did he know what it was, he also knew what it meant.

"Who wants you to do that?"

"My attorney."

"Your attorney?" he raised an eyebrow.

"Why do you have an attorney, and why is he telling you to get a prenup?"

Be careful of what you say here, she reminded herself. "I have some assets that I need to keep the ownership of."

"What kind of assets?" Jerome asked a fair question and Tammy wanted to give him some sort of answer that made sense *and* wasn't a lie.

"Like an inheritance that I don't want to be claimed as joint property."

"*Like* an inheritance, so it's not really an inheritance?" Tammy was hoping he wouldn't catch that qualifying word "like." It would have been easier on everyone if his ears would have missed that and just absorbed that word right into the other ones. It was the closest and most honest answer she could give. She couldn't say winnings, or money. *Wait, wait, Lord thank you.* She had just been handed a lifeline.

"Well, it's real close to an inheritance, but it's not technically called that."

"Tammy, just level with me, what is it then?"

"It's some property."

"Property. What, is it a million-dollar mansion you've got hidden in River Oaks, that you don't want me to know about? So you're a millionaire?" he joked.

"No, no," she laughed. *Lord, I just answered the first question,* she quietly explained to the Lord.

"O.K., so where is this mystery property and how did you get it?"

O.K. Lord, he's assuming it's real estate so that's what I'll let him continue to think. I guess these are legitimate questions but he needs to chill. She didn't know if he was asking out of concern or being nosey. "It's close, and that's where the inheritance thing comes into play."

He thought for a minute, noting her secrecy. "Is that all?"

"Yes, that's it."

"You sure?"

"Yes, I'm sure."

"O.K. fine."

She studied him. He seemed to be O.K. with it. His words said he was and his body language seemed to parallel them but she still wasn't done. She had to get him to sign it.

She smiled at him. "Thank you."

He shook his head, without saying a word.

Tammy pushed on. "I have it here it you want to look at it. And if you're O.K. with it, we can take care of it now." She tried to sound as nice and non-threatening as she could.

"Is that what's in that envelope?" his eyes pointed to it.

"Yes," she reached for it and pulled the stapled sheets of paper out and handed it to him.

His eyes slowly moved across the top of the page, then down each line. She watched. She could tell he was no longer reading every word. He started skimming lines, then quickly jumping paragraphs and turning pages. "Tammy, there's no property address listed."

"I know, but that doesn't matter."

"What do you mean, it doesn't matter?"

"I mean it's not important, is it? Will you change your mind if you saw it?"

"Probably not, it's yours, but there's a lot of big lawyer words in this long document," he flipped through the pages while creases formed in his forehead. "This is saying a lot for just one property."

"We can go talk to the lawyer and he can explain anything you have a question about."

"I need to look over all this first."

Tammy tried to cover her disappointment. "How long do you think that will take, a couple hours?"

"Huh, no. I don't want to rush through this. I have to take my time. Why does it seem like you're rushing me?"

"I don't mean to, I just thought we could take care of it today and start planning for the wedding." She shrugged her shoulders.

"Tammy, you just dropped this on me out of the blue. You've never, once, said anything about this, or given me any clue that this is what you brought me over here to do. I need some time...to think, to look at this."

"I understand. Take all the time you need. Just don't take too long," she lightheartedly leaned over and jabbed his waist. "Because I can't wait to marry you," she smiled.

Jerome smiled back but didn't say anything in response. He just stood and pulled her up toward him and hugged her like he was soothing a child that had just made a big mistake.

She didn't know what to think of his hug but she didn't have much time to think further because he quickly let go and simply kissed her on the forehead before turning toward the door, with the contract clenched in one hand. He held up the envelope like he was showing her he still had it in his possession and without looking back he shut the door behind him without uttering a word.

Chapter 28

The Introduction

TONIGHT THE LOTTERY pool would meet Tammy's fiancé. Not that she was seeking their approval of Jerome, she just wanted to see what they thought of him and since everyone wanted to go out anyway, this was a great opportunity. She also didn't want to be seen alone at a restaurant with all couples and it get back to him. He might question why she would go to a couples' dinner without him. She was also reluctant to bring him because their group was going to spend a decent amount of money on appetizers and drinks and she wasn't sure what he would make of it all. She definitely would have to tailor down her order to make sure their portion of the check was reasonable because she was no longer allowed to pick up the tab; he had made that requirement clear. So she would have to be mindful of the bill she would be racking up. If she had come by herself there would be no issue, but she certainly didn't want him thinking she wasted money. It's not the time to be frivolous with money, spending it on restaurant meals with your friends when you're in the middle of planning a wedding. Of course, this is what Jerome would be thinking, and that was all fine with Tammy.

They arrived at the steak house and were ushered into a private room where everyone was already seated and chatting. After introducing Jerome to everyone and everyone to him, they sat near the end of the solid wood table, Jerome beside Craig. It wasn't long before the room's noise level began to rise once more as the multiple conversations were filled with laughter and outbursts, the sounds of not having a care in the world.

Jerome took inventory of this group and tried to denote what they all had in common. He knew they all went to the same church, his church, but it seemed odd how close they all were to each other when it seemed like they were an unlikely group. You had an older Hispanic couple, a Caucasian couple, a Black couple, a mixed couple, and a young black woman. This was the oddest group of people he'd ever seen, and it was wonderful. It still didn't make sense to Jerome how a young single woman fit into this group of all married couples though. He thought maybe they all grew close attending a new membership class at church or something. They had such great energy and seemed more like family than friends.

Jerome shared small talk with Craig but mostly talked with Tammy. Orders of appetizers and drinks came to the table. There was so much food, he wasn't sure if anyone would actually be ordering a main dish. There were piles of food on each oversized plate, all lined up in the middle of the table. One plate had chicken tenders, quail, and alligator with a variety of sauces to choose from, another plate had only onion rings, a third fried okra and fried green tomatoes, and still another, a seafood tray filled with fried shrimp, scallops, and calamari which was duplicated in two other spots on the table. The last plate housed loaded potato skins. All that food, and that's not even counting the standard baskets of rolls they normally start you off with. Then the drinks were distributed, Mango Mojito, Maui Margarita, a pint of draft beer, Lagers and Ales and a few sodas and teas were also included. Jerome didn't know what half of the drinks were but he did know they weren't cheap. Already seeing that this would be a hefty bill, he leaned over to Tammy and asked how it would be split and she reassured him that they would have a separate bill from everyone else. She told Jerome that she had already explained to the group beforehand that they were on a budget and were saving up for the wedding and all that comes with it.

Jerome studied everyone. Maria and Jorge, he assumed, had been married the longest. They were so comfortable with each other that they said whatever. She had just scolded Jorge for getting more onion rings and proclaimed that would be more pounds he'd be adding to the ones he still needed to get rid of. Maria didn't care who was in the room as she patted her husband's stomach. Jorge was unconcerned, and kept eating.

Don and Janet, if Jerome remembered their names correctly, seemed to act too polite to each other. They acted happy and laughed with the group but there was something about their smiles; they didn't seem genuine. Not that they were hiding something, but that their smiles were painted on to cover up for an earlier argument or something. And they seemed to act with caution. Jerome noticed that they hadn't touched each other. All the other couples were leaning on each other or playfully jabbing each other in the side and talking about any and everything. Don and Janet were more reserved, even when the appetizer platters were handed down the table, Jerome noticed that Janet ware careful not to let her hand touch Don's. *That's interesting,* Jerome thought.

Craig and Amanda seemed to be enjoying themselves a great deal, although Amanda called for the waiter a couple times to get her drink exactly the way she wanted it and asked for a few condiments that didn't come on the platters.

Frank and Laura seemed to be just having fun, enjoying each other's company and the comradery of the entire group. Jerome noticed how Frank lovingly squeezed his wife and touched her hand as she giggled at whatever he was saying under his breath.

Jerome held Tammy's hand under the table, satisfied that she hung out with such outgoing and sensible people, no matter how the group was formed, or how she became part of it.

"So Jerome," Don put his glass down, "What do you do for a living?"

"I'm in construction. I'm a foreman."

"Is that right?"

"Yes. My crew has been part of a lot of building projects. They do mostly masonry and sheetrock."

"Masonry?" Amanda looked at Craig.

"Brick laying," Craig answered before Jerome could.

"Local?" Frank asked.

"Mostly. I used to travel to other states and do some work here and there but Texas has kept me pretty busy."

"So what kind of buildings?" Janet was sincere in her question.

"Pretty much anything, there's no job too small or too big."

"Anything, we would know?"

"Absolutely. We did renovations to the George R. Brown Convention Center, Heritage Plaza, JPMorgan Chase Tower...Did you know that's the tallest building in the city? It's over a thousand feet tall. Let's see, Rice University, and Minute Maid Park. Even though I was young, I still remember marveling at the sight of that building, I don't know if it was because the Astros played there or what. Of course it was called Enron Field back then—"

"Please don't say that word. That's a sore spot at our house." Jerome looked at Don then Janet, who rolled her eyes. Jorge tried to smooth things over. "Well, I remember when they were in the Astrodome."

"That was before my time. But a little story on Minute Maid, you know that train at the top, during one of the renovations, I got a chance to go up there and touch it."

"That's high," Maria's eyes widened.

"Yes, but there are steps that go up there and I had a safety harness on for extra protection so I was alright."

"How neat."

"So what was the most interesting thing you've built?"

"Most interesting? I'm not sure."

"Oh, what did you like building the most?"

"Schools, we've built a lot of them. And the population in Houston just keeps growing and growing. We can't keep up."

"And the least?"

"I tell you what, we've built a number of prisons, that's what I don't like. Sometimes, I wonder how many kids that go to one of the schools we built, will wind up in prison." He should his head. "I think the taxpayers' money could be better spent on youth programs to prevent kids from going down that path but it seems like the government would rather spend it on incarceration."

"So what project are you most looking forward to doing?"

"That's easy," he looked at Tammy, "building a house for this beautiful woman here."

Tammy gasped and buried her head in his chest.

Oohs and aahs were spread around the room. Craig gave him a fist pump, "Good one, man." Everyone laughed.

"So how did you two meet?"

Jerome looked at Tammy. "I had been watching her for a while at church. Then I finally saw her outside of church, at the mall, and decided to approach her."

"Was it love at first sight?"

"Not for Tammy, it was fear at first sight."

"What do you mean?" Tammy turned her body to face him.

"I saw you clutch your purse," Jerome looked up, "She thought I was gonna rob her."

Tammy's mouth opened and her cheeks turned bright red.

"Tammy, you did?"

"Yes, he was just staring at me and then he started running my way. I didn't know him."

The room fell out laughing so, that Tammy had to laugh herself.

"I was only trying to give her my number."

The evening went on with laughter and exchanges of stories. Jerome had a good time and felt everyone genuinely wanted to get to know him. These people were down to Earth and real and he liked that. He could be himself, have stimulating conversation, and just have fun. And Tammy was enjoying herself as well, that was the most important thing.

As the evening came to a close, the bills were given out to each couple. Under normal circumstances, they would get one big bill and one couple would pay, after all, even as large as the bill normally is, it was just like paying for a happy meal to a millionaire, but since Jerome was in attendance, they didn't want to put any pressure on him to feel obligated at a future time, nor did they want him to wonder how one couple would be so willing to pay for everyone else. So they felt it best to play it safe.

"Well everyone, it's been great as usual. Jerome, it was nice to meet you. We look forward to having you around more often," Frank extended his hand.

"Thank you, I had a ball. I really did. You guys are crazy. And I like it."

Hugs and handshakes were exchanged and everyone parted ways. And Tammy's smile couldn't be erased.

Chapter 29

Moment of Truth

IT HAD BEEN weeks since Tammy first mentioned anything about a prenup. She didn't want to pressure Jerome, she wanted him to take his time and get used to the idea. He had looked the agreement over but now he wanted to meet with the lawyer as well to get his questions answered and the appointment was today.

Tammy looked at her watch again and started to feel uneasy. Her eyes raced back and forth to several points in the building's lobby but she didn't see him. Jerome should have been here by now. They only had five more minutes before they were supposed to meet with the lawyer. *Had he forgotten? Not hardly.* They had talked this morning and again when they were both on their way so him not being here was unsettling. *Had he changed his mind?* Tammy was already taken aback because Jerome didn't want to drive over there together, he had insisted on meeting her. She wasn't sure what that meant, if anything.

Their phone conversations since the day she had told him about her wanting a prenup had been rather normal but she felt like he was somehow guarded, nothing like how he acted at dinner when he met everyone, and she had even told him so. His response was that he felt like she didn't trust him. Tammy tried to reassure him that it was definitely not the case and she hoped this meeting would put all his reservations to rest so they could move forward with their wedding plans.

She repositioned herself in the chair and pulled her phone out of her purse to call him. Before she could push send she saw him rushing toward her. She stood to meet him.

"Sorry, a traffic jam came out of nowhere. I should have been here."

She studied his eyes to see if she could tell what he was thinking, but couldn't. "It's O.K. I'm just glad you came," Tammy's smile was really a plea. When she looked down she noticed he was holding a binder.

"O.K. I'm following you," were the only words he said next, as they were already late, so Tammy took her cue and headed for the elevators. The silence was deafening even with other people crammed in the square box. Since they weren't alone Tammy didn't know what to say. She wanted to ask him what he planned to discuss with the lawyer but she certainly couldn't do it now. And conjuring up small talk seemed like a facade, like they were just avoiding talking about the elephant in the room. She wanted him to say something, anything, but the only sound came from the ding signaling their selected floor had arrived. She would have to wait until they got inside to hear what was coming next.

"Good afternoon," the receptionist greeted them as they walked through the doors. "Who are you here to see?"

"Mr. Roberts."

"Yes, he's expecting you, go right on in."

They both walked into the lawyer's open door and exchanged greetings and salutations. He directed them to the table and they all sat. Mr. Roberts started first. "So Mr. Davis, I hear you have some questions about the prenuptial agreement that Ms. Chapman would like you to sign."

"Of course," Jerome took the documents out of his binder and asked Mr. Roberts to explain a few terms and how they applied in the situation. Tammy sat quietly while Jerome took notes. She tried to read his body language and listened at the inflection in his voice. She wasn't sure if his intensity was him being thorough or if he was trying to uncover some ulterior motives he thought she may have.

"Mr. Davis many couples get a prenup. It's not uncommon. And because one party asks for one doesn't mean they don't trust you."

"And why can't we just discuss this after we get married?"

"Well a postnuptial mainly pertains to joint assets. Basically here's our money and this is what we want to do with it. You can add stipulations for if one spouse cheats—"

"I was talking about a will, just putting it in a will," Jerome jumped in.

"A will wouldn't be sufficient in this case. Say something happens to you and you become incapacitated. Well your family could contest that Tammy's property is joint property and they could win the right to make her liquidate it to pay for the medical costs of keeping you alive indefinitely, whether the doctors feel like you would get better or not. There's a lot of emotion that comes into play here and Tammy could potentially have no control over her own property. Medical costs could deplete her assets. The courts will look at *your* joint assets, they won't look at your family's. This prenup will protect Tammy's property from ever being considered." He paused to let the information sink in. "This may sound cold, I'm not saying that Tammy wouldn't do anything she could to keep you alive but parents, siblings, they can be irrational and want to keep you alive no matter what's at stake. Even if the doctor says you'll just be a vegetable, most parents will still hang on to hope or they just can't see themselves pulling the plug."

"But that would be up to Tammy to do."

"Mr. Davis. Most married couples don't get a will done until years after they're married. And even if you were to get one, your family can protest it, especially if something happens early in the marriage and they can convince the court that you two haven't been married long enough for her to make such a decision…I've seen some really messed up cases over the years. I've even seen some advanced directives be protested, they have loop holes too."

"Will the property ever be joint property?"

"You will be able to enjoy the property together as a married couple, but if you ever divorce, the property will remain hers and will not be considered in the settlement. That means you essentially can't get the value of it, or any increase in value it may rise to, and split it in half. It will all go to Tammy."

Jerome looked at Tammy. "And what do your parents think about this prenup?"

Tammy hesitated. "They don't know anything about it. I haven't told them because it's really none of their business. This is between you and me."

Jerome thought about that. So it wasn't her parents that didn't trust him, it was all her.

Mr. Roberts broke in to try and ease Jerome's doubts. "Mr. Davis if you're still thinking that Tammy is doing this because she doesn't trust you, think of it from her perspective. She's the one that has something to lose. And she may also be thinking, if he trusts me he shouldn't have a problem signing, and why would you not sign unless you potentially have some hidden motive yourself?"

Jerome leaned back in his chair and looked at Tammy. "You know I showed Barbara this contract and let her read over it." Tammy's eye brows lifted. "She must really like you because I left it with her and she called me a couple days later and told me she was surprised by it, but didn't see a problem with it." Tammy's expression softened. "I don't really agree with this, I mean I'm not thrilled about it at all. This is something rich people do and I don't think it's necessary but," he grabbed the pen and turned to the last page and scribbled his signature, "if this is what you think you need, fine. I don't want to take anything from you." And with that he handed the papers to the lawyer, told Tammy bye and walked out of the office."

Chapter 30

Changes

DON HEARD THE garage door open signaling Janet was now home from work. He quickly gathered up his papers and put them aside then got up from the couch and sat at the kitchen table to wait for her to enter. He thought about meeting Janet at the door and giving her a kiss but he wasn't sure she would accept it. He would have to wait and see what her demeanor would be. She dropped her keys into the kitchen drawer, said hello with no inflection in her voice nor smile on her face, and walked toward the bedroom.

Don said a quick prayer then patiently waited for Janet to return. After returning, Janet headed straight for the cabinet and started to take out pots and pans and a pack of chicken from the refrigerator. Don is reminded of all the times his wife has made dinner over the years, for their entire family. Their two grown children were out of the house but she still took care of him. "I'd like to take you out for dinner tonight." He waited for a response.

"I appreciate it but no thank you." Her words weren't tarnished with madness nor sarcasm, she was polite, too polite, and that concerned Don. She responded to him like he was a colleague at the office, like she was giving him a professional courtesy. If she had been sad or maybe even a little dramatic, he'd be able to handle that. But this response was so void of emotion, it was like she didn't really care one way or the other. He didn't like this, what they had become nor the atmosphere in their home. It was like they were distant roommates not husband and wife. How had it come to this? When did the passion and joy leave his wife's heart? Was he the sole reason? Had he really lost sight of their marriage and the woman he had fallen in love with?

His heart began to ache and he remembered what the counselor had told him, to concentrate on her needs and fight for their marriage. He reached for a book from the counter and opened it up to the placeholder. "Will you sit down for a minute? I want to read something to you."

She washed her hands and without a word came to the table. She kept her gaze intently on his, as if she were sitting down to meet with her boss. Don really looked at his wife. She was more beautiful now than when they had first met. He didn't think that was even possible. Her face was more mature, surrounded by long layers of brown hair that showcased the purest sapphire eyes. Eyes that once held shimmer for him, now only seemed piercing and cold. Janet had built a wall between them, where she kept her emotions safely hidden away, protected even from her husband. He was at a loss for words, guilt ridden that it had come to this, but he was going to try and make a first step, so he read...

How beautiful you are, my darling, how beautiful you are! Your eyes are like doves behind your veil;

Your hair is like a flock of goats that have descended from Mount Gilead. Your teeth are like a flock of newly shorn ewes which have come up from their washing, all of which bear twins, and not one among them has lost her young. Your lips are like a scarlet thread, and your mouth is lovely. Your temples are like a slice of a pomegranate. Your two breasts are like two fawns, twins of a gazelle which feed among the lilies. You are altogether beautiful, my darling, and there is no blemish in you.

You have made my heart beat faster, my sister, my bride; you have made my heart beat faster with a single glance of your eyes, with a single strand of your necklace. How beautiful is your love, my sister, my bride! How much better is your love than wine, and the fragrance of your oils than all kinds of spices! Your lips, my bride, drip honey; Honey and milk are under your tongue, and the fragrance of your garments is like the fragrance of Lebanon. A garden locked is my sister, my bride, a rock garden locked, a spring sealed up. Your shoots are an orchard of pomegranates with choice fruits, henna with nard plants, nard and saffron, calamus and cinnamon, with all the trees of frankincense, myrrh and aloes, along with all the finest spices. You are a garden spring, a well of fresh water, and streams flowing from Lebanon.

Awake, O north wind, and come, wind of the south; Make my garden breathe out fragrance, let its spices be wafted abroad. May my beloved come into his garden and eat its choice fruits!

Don looked up, being finished, and leaned back in his chair waiting for Janet to respond. After an uncomfortably long pause, she said, "Yes, I'm familiar with that passage."

"The counselor suggested I do something...well, I was trying to show you how much I cared."

"I asked you to pay more attention to me, to make me feel cherished, to take the time and show me that you're serious about changing and giving me what I need."

"What do you think I'm doing?"

"Those aren't your words. You did what was convenient. You took the easy way out. Can't you find something good to say about me without quoting the Bible? That wasn't from your heart."

Don's face began to turn red. Janet noticed but didn't care. Pastor David had taught a bible study lesson not too long ago on romantic Bible passages so all Don had to do was look at his notes and pull this out. That was not good enough. If he didn't take the time, and make the effort, she was going to call him out on it. She was tired of him doing things the way he wanted to, quick and easy, just to say he had done it, like he was checking off a to-do list. She was no longer going to pretend, no longer hold back, nor protect his ego. She had done that long enough. After all, he said he'd do whatever it took, so there was no time to sugarcoat things.

"Do you know how long it took me to find this?"

Janet dismissed the fact that all he had to do was look at the Table of Contents and find the book. "Look, you're missing the point. You could have chosen any number of poems in there that Solomon wrote. I don't want to hear what someone else wrote to their wife. I want to hear what my own husband thinks about me."

Don shot up from the table. He couldn't keep his frustration bottled up any longer. "Fine." He didn't know what else to say and he didn't want to say the wrong thing so he marched to the counter, grabbed his keys, and stormed out of the house.

Just as soon as he was gone, a light flicked on in Janet's mind. She was now so aware of what she had just done. She walked over to the now empty seat Don had occupied just moments ago, and sat rehearsing what had just happened, in her mind. She moved the Bible, still open to the passage Don had just read, closer to her. She reread the passage and cried. Out of panic she called the counselor's cell phone and he answered after several rings.

"This is Dr. Collins."

"Dr. Collins, this is Janet. I just hurt Don's feelings." She brought him up to speed on what just took place and waited for a response.

"Janet, you've got to appreciate where he's at. He's making an attempt. He's not where you want him to be but he's making an effort and you just shot him down, which may discourage him from trying."

"O.K." She sighed.

"Think of him as a baby. You wouldn't expect a baby to walk before he crawled."

"I understand where you're going with this but he should know these things already. He did them when we first got married, even before we were married. Why do you think I fell in love with him in the first place?"

"People change and sometimes need to be reminded. Ease into telling him what you need. But before you can do that, you need to appreciate and acknowledge what he's doing already, even if it seems small. You need to find something that you can praise him for every day."

"I can't stroke his ego."

"Janet, if you want to have the chance of making this work, he's got to feel like he's making some progress or he'll get discouraged and stop trying because he'll think that nothing he does will please you."

"We'll see. I can't make any promises."

"All I ask is that you'll try." And with that Janet thanked him for his time and they hung up.

Chapter 31

Joy Bells

ALL THE WOMEN were sitting on the couches in Maria's living room mulling over wedding books and magazines, the air full of excitement. Maria had insisted on them coming over her house verses Tammy's apartment saying, "you don't need to worry about entertaining us, just worry about the wedding." And Tammy was grateful. Anything that looked nice, they showed Tammy and if she liked it, they'd write the information on it, tear out the page and set it aside for her to go through later. Tammy was busy on her tablet, researching venues for the reception. She and Jerome had decided to have the wedding at church but the fellowship hall would be too small for a reception, well at least not the one Tammy envisioned. Besides, Tammy was looking for a place that would fit the elegance she was going for. She wanted tablecloths and china, and a lot more. This was an opportunity of a lifetime, to plan your own wedding with no financial restrictions, and she wanted it to be all she had dreamed of.

"Well I guess he signed the prenup?" Amanda asked.

"Yes, how did that go?" Laura joined in.

"It was kind of shaky there for a while. He asked fair questions but I was uneasy the whole time. I still feel guilty."

"Don't be, men do this type of stuff all the time."

"You did the right thing."

"Yep, he'll get over it."

The encouraging words came from everyone but Tammy explained further. "I know but he gave me this look like he was trying to figure me out or something. Like he knew I wasn't being totally honest. He eventually signed it but left right away. We didn't talk for a couple days after that."

"Well what did he say when you finally talked?" Laura flipped another page.

"He said he just needed a day or so to wrap his mind around it. Then he asked if there were any more surprises." Giggles and laughter sprung forth because of the irony that Tammy was going to give Jerome the biggest surprise yet. She would eventually have to tell him about the lottery money but that could be years from now. "Then he said he was over it, that he trusts me, even though it seems I don't trust him yet, and let's move forward."

Heads nodded in satisfaction.

"So with the plans you've shared with us on this wedding and everything you want to do, how are you going to explain spending this much money?" Before Tammy could utter anything Amanda clarified, "Wait, forget about Jerome for a second, what about your parents?" Amanda asked a valid question.

"My dad won't be an issue. He may comment about how we really went all out on the wedding but that'll be it. I planned some things with my mom like the guest list and the gown—Eeeh!" Tammy shrieked. "Let me show you."

"You already found a gown?"

"Yes, and it's beautiful! I love it. I found it at a boutique in The Galleria. I just have to get it altered a little." After a few swipes on the screen, Tammy turned her tablet around to show everyone the picture of the dress she had chosen. Just seeing it heightened the emotions around the room.

"This is absolutely gorgeous. How much is it?"

"About three thousand."

"Tammy, yikes!"

"For that amount of money you should be able to press a button and it alter itself," Amanda joked.

"Pass that over here so I can get a good look." Maria studied the picture of a model wearing a full length lace gown with a commanding train, and sparkles of light shown in what seemed like every inch, even down to the trim of the sleeves. "I've never seen anything like it," she shook her head, "Tammy this is beautiful."

"Thank you. I know it's expensive but you only get married once right? I had to tell the lady who waited on us not to tell my mom any prices, and to just say it was all taken care of. I started to go there before hand and pick out what I wanted, but I really wanted to share that memory with her, so she won't feel left out, but I can't plan this stuff with her." Tammy gestured her hand over all the pictures and notes. "She'd ask me why in the world am I spending all this money on one day and where is it all coming from."

"What will she say when she see's everything *at* the wedding?"

"She'll just think his parents paid for it."

"What will you tell Jerome?"

216

"I don't know; I haven't gotten that far yet," Tammy slumped back on the couch, "If I tell him my parents paid for it, he'll try and thank them and then they'll tell him they thought his parents paid for it. I don't want to lie to him anyway. If I tell him it's all been taken care of he'll assume it's from my parents but the end result will be the same, he'll find out that's not the case."

"Well, if he's anything like my husband," Laura chimed in, "he's not gonna want his future father-in-law to spend a lot for a wedding. He'd actually want to pay for it himself."

"Speaking of that, Jerome told me to just tell him how much everything costs so he could make sure I have it."

"Huh, that's not gonna work."

"What if you just tell him a figure that you think he'll be happy with? You're paying for the rest anyway." Maria shrugged her shoulders.

"That's a good idea, I can give him a range like, let's say twenty thousand."

"Noooo, you'd better bring that down. You only have a few months for him to save up, unless he's already been saving."

"Yes, you don't want to overwhelm him."

The conversation was interrupted by Tammy's cell phone. "That's him now," she whispered, getting up to go outside to answer.

"Ask him how much he wants to spend."

"Just ask for a total budget."

"O.K., O.K.," Tammy swiped the phone with her thumb.

"Hi," she closed the door behind her, "just looking at wedding stuff with the ladies."

"O.K. I just wanted to see when we can go look at some rings. I found a few places," Jerome said.

217

"Tomorrow, if that's not too early."

She could hear the smile in his voice. "That's just fine."

"I have a question. How much were you looking to spend on the wedding?" Tammy listened intently.

"Whatever we need to; I mean, I don't want to go crazy because a lot of that stuff doesn't really matter."

Doesn't matter? Tammy uncrossed her legs. Before she could say anything, he interjected, "I mean, I've been to some weddings where…all of that wasn't necessary. People spend all that money for one day. We just need to have fun. We can ask our mom's to cook a dish, my dad can barbeque, Barbara can make some sweet potato pies and 7-up cakes…"

This is not a family reunion. Tammy tried to keep her composure. "That sounds nice but I actually want something more formal, and elegant, a sit down dinner with tablecloths and silverware."

"How much is that gonna cost?"

"I don't know yet. I'm looking at a few places that I like. How much is the wedding budget?"

"My parents got married and spent less than a thousand on everything, and they're still together."

Are you serious? You want to have our wedding in a barn or something? Tammy tried to keep calm. "Yes, but that was over thirty years ago. Times have changed. It costs more to have a wedding nowadays."

"I don't want to spend too much. We've eventually got to think about getting a down payment for a house. I was serious about building you one. I have all the contacts I need to get it done, unless of course you want to live in that secret property of yours." *Jab noted.* "And one of us will have to break our lease on our apartment. Yours is nicer but I'd have you move in with me, but I know mine might not be up to your standards. But I really want us to find something together until we're ready to build, so that would mean we'd be breaking two leases."

"I understand all that but I want this day to be special. Keep that in mind. So what's the budget?" Tammy pressed.

"I'd say around six or seven thousand max."

Tammy didn't say a word. She was too busy calculating everything she wanted to do. It was a fair amount but she knew with everything she had planned, she'd be happy to get away with spending fifty thousand. She already knew she would be fine with whatever amount he came up with, that wasn't the issue, because she would pay for everything over his budget anyway. The problem was she knew once he saw her creation, he'd know it cost way more than what he allotted. But she would have to cross that bridge when she got to it. Right now she just wanted to make him feel like she was on board with his plans. "That's a nice amount. I can definitely handle that."

"I'm glad. I'll see you later. And have fun but don't let your friends influence you to spend more than what we've agreed on."

"Don't worry, they won't." And with that, they said their good-byes.

Chapter 32

New Day

LAURA PICKED UP the phone to call her sister. She wanted to make sure Nell wasn't also coming up with ideas on how to get a cut of their parents' money. She would rather have talked to them both at the same time by a three-way phone conversation but that might trigger warning bells in both of their minds and one may feed off of the other and suspect that Laura had something to do with the money in the first place. She could have talked to each of them individually and in person, that would have been ideal but she couldn't stand to even look at Maury and she was sure he hated her guts right now anyway. Nell claimed she had been so busy with her kids' activities she didn't have time to meet face-to-face. So now Laura sat about to call both of them to try and persuade them to leave their parents' money alone, without sounding overbearing or suspicious.

The phone rang twice and Nell picked up. "Hey, what's going on with you?" Laura could hear her niece and nephew playing in the background.

"Did I catch you at a good time?"

"Just as good as any, what's going on?"

"I called to talk to you about Mamma and Daddy."

"What's wrong?"

"You know what Maury pulled, right?"

"Yes, he went overboard with that."

"Wait, what do you mean by overboard?"

"He took advantage. He should have just asked for just enough to get him something decent. I don't know if I agree with what you did but I do understand why you did it."

"Well, I don't think we have the right to be asking our parents for *any* amount of money. We're all grown and made the decisions we did and it's not fair for us to ask them for anything at their stage in life. They were blessed to get that money no matter where it came from. I believe it's a miracle actually. And they are the ones that need to enjoy it. So hopefully you agree with me that we won't try and ask them for any of it."

There was a long pause. "Laura, that's easy for you to say, you don't have any children. Do you realize how much it takes to raise a child? Sometimes surprises happen. Sometimes people need a little help and I don't think there's anything wrong with asking family for help if you need it."

"Nell, you knew the responsibility of being a parent before you decided to do it. And since you know emergencies come up, you should prepare for them. Why should our parents have to be prepared for your emergency, or mine, or Maury's? They raised us in a totally different time and they still made it. There are so many more opportunities to get ahead these days. You and I can get a better job if we need to. We don't have to go through half the stuff they did. I don't get it, why would you put that burden on them?"

"Look Laura, I'm not saying that I'll ask for anything, but if they offer, I'm not going to refuse it."

"Great, that's reassuring," Laura couldn't believe she'd have to watch out for her sister too. Nell would probably hint around that her kids needed school clothes or something, because she knew how much their mom couldn't resist anything when it came to her grandkids.

"You sure are being over protective, why is that?"

"I just told you why and you should be over protective too, it's both of our parents. We should be happy for them, not trying to take from them."

"Right…well I'll have to talk to you later, I've got to go."

"Alright, bye." Laura didn't know what else to say and she wondered if Nell had already tried to get to their parents. She couldn't give it much thought though because she wanted to get this next call over with. She had to call Maury.

This call would be a roll of the dice because she had no idea if he would answer or not. Either way she was going to get her point across whether talking directly to him or by leaving a message.

"What do you want?"

"Well, hello to you too." He was still mad but Laura didn't care; he had it coming.

"What you did was foul."

"No, what *you* did was foul. I'm only looking out for our parents but you're only looking out for yourself. And I'm telling you, don't try that stuff again."

"You need to stay out of people's business."

"You need to grow up, Maury. Don't you see that you're draining them? I shouldn't have to protect my parents from my own brother."

"Man, I was going to pay for that SUV."

"At what point are you going to realize that it's not all about you? Look, you're my brother and I do love you but I'm not going to let you take advantage of our parents, so you can stay mad at me. I don't care."

The click in her ear was all she heard. Laura pulled the phone down from the side of her face to see if he'd really hung up on her and the words "call ended" were her verification.

Maury's attitude didn't faze her. She wasn't about to let him get away with his underhanded tricks so she showed him a few tricks of her own. Shortly after getting off the phone with the lawyer, two days after Maury's stunt, Laura went over to her parents' house and talked to her dad. She apologized for anything disrespectful she had said and the way she had stormed out of their house. He leveled with Laura and told her about his concerns but he felt helpless since Maggy had already finalized everything before he even knew what had happened. Laura had asked to see the contract and after almost falling to the floor, she pointed out a few tricks that the dealership had hidden in the contract. The contract stated that if the payment was late even one time during the eighteen months of 0 percent interest, the interest would increase to prime plus 2.9 percent. There was no grace period and the payment had to be received before close of business the day it was due. So if Maury was even a day late, or even a minute after that day's closing deadline, anytime within that year and a half, they would start the interest. On top of that, they assessed fees if they received a late payment. The only thing her mom had focused on was the 2.9 percent (after the eighteen months at 0%) but when you add that to the prime, the interest was really at 7.4. But that wasn't all. In fine print at the bottom it declared that this was a subprime contract and the consumer would need to add a minimum of 10 percent more to the interest up to 12 percent max at the discretion of the dealership dependent upon factors including but not limited to: length of loan, credit rating, and number of late payments.

"So basically Maury has gotten you into a variable interest loan that can go as high as 29% if he makes just one late payment."

"Oh my God," Laura remembered how Tom had dropped his head in his hands.

"Well, Maury said he looked at all the paperwork and that everything looked good. I don't know what to say." Laura had almost felt sorry for her mom but her anger for Maury overruled any sympathy.

She also explained what the attorney had told her about Texas' 3-day right to cancel law which gave you the right to cancel a purchase if the transaction is made somewhere other than the seller's place of business. And since the salesman came to her parents' home to get Maggy to sign the paperwork, it qualified. Maury's over zealousness had actually worked in their parents' favor. Now they didn't have to plea with the dealership to reverse the transaction and hope they would take pity on the situation. They had legal grounds to return the vehicle and get all the money back, every red cent. All Laura and her dad had to do was convince Maggy to agree to take the SUV back. Laura found the Notice of Cancellation form buried in all the paperwork, one thing the salesman did right, and Tom got Maggy to sign it. Laura already had a tow truck on stand-bye.

***

Janet awakened to the smell of bacon and walked in the kitchen to find Don finishing up a nice breakfast he had prepared. He fixed her plate and set it on the table in her usual spot. She smiled and told him thank you and he sat across from her.

She had noticed he was trying. He has made a point to sit with her while she watched TV and put his arm around her. Even when she watched Lifetime, he sat there, through the whole movie. It didn't even matter to her that he fell asleep most of the time. Just the fact that he was there with her, he was making an effort to spend time with *her*, not his job.

They ate in silence for the most part, a little small talk about what's going on in the news but that was about it. Don didn't mind though. He was satisfied that they were actually eating together. That was a start, he hoped. He finished first and started cleaning up the mess, wiping down the counters and placing the pots and pans in the dishwasher.

"I've got to head out for work."

Janet, still eating, looked up. "O.K. Breakfast was really nice. I had forgotten how well you can cook." They exchanged smiles. "Thank you for taking the time to fix it. It really made my day."

Don nodded. It was too much to try and give her a hug or anything so he simply said "you're welcome," gathered his things, and headed out the door.

Not too long after Don left, Janet also finished up her morning routine and headed for her car. After cuing up the house alarm she locked the door to the garage, pressed the garage door opener and walked around and opened the driver's side door. She placed her purse inside then reached to pick up an envelope off of her seat. Thinking it to be mail she had dropped, she dismissed it by moving it to the passenger seat beside her purse, then backed out of the garage and waited for the door to close.

Having a few seconds to spare, Janet wanted to see what kind of mail she had overlooked. Was it a bill or junk mail? To her surprise it wasn't mail at all. She held it, a blank envelope with "My Wife" written on the front. *That's strange, he's never left me a note before,* she thought. Instead of opening it right away, she contemplated what could be in it. Had he finally gotten a divorce decree? *But he just made me breakfast,* she reasoned with herself. *Maybe that was his good-bye gesture.* Her mind went back and forth. What if it's the bill for the counseling sessions? She already told him she wasn't going back and didn't care what happened next. She told him she was done and it didn't matter to her one bit if he continued to see the counselor or not. *If he expects me to pay for that session that I walked out on, he's sadly mistaken.*

She tore the envelope open, ready for anything her husband might have snuck in there. She unfolded the paper and realized it wasn't an invoice at all, and it wasn't divorce papers. It was a…letter. Her eyes quickly scanned the entire paper and glanced at his ending. Where his signature would have been, he simply wrote, Your Husband. This was no "Dear John" letter. Janet discovered that it wasn't a letter at all, it was a poem. *Don wrote me a poem? A poem? Interesting.* She held her breath and began to read:

Our Love

Baby girl
You are my entire world
You're asking all these questions
Like I'm supposed to make a confession

Things like, will you love me through sickness and health?
Will you be here when I'm not here for myself?
But I want you to know
You're my only goal
My love for you is bulletproof
No one can go around or through
No one can get inside my head
Because I think of you every night before bed
If you leave I'd lose my mind
The one I can already not find

Janet couldn't help but giggle. Then she continued reading.

There will be battles ahead of us
But that's life, we can't put up a fuss
I need you with me
Without you I can no longer see
You're so bright
You're my little light
You will always be mine
You don't know how much you mean to me
Because in my heart there's a lock and you have the key

Love, Your Husband

PS: Yes, I wrote this myself

Janet sat there, stunned. He had never done anything like this before. This was not her husband. For once, he didn't try to find something quick so he could just say he completed a task. Unlike his earlier Bible recitation, he created something of his own. He actually took the time to do something special, something just for her. A flood of tears was all she could gather in response.

Chapter 33

Sparkle

JEROME PULLED UP to another jewelry store and Tammy hoped she'd find something she liked in this one. This was the last order of business before the wedding and he was eager to get it over with. The store was pretty big, with rows of encased jewelry, quite an impressive selection. The man behind the counter greeted them and welcomed them to look around; pointing to some catalogues they could also look through if they didn't find what they liked in the store. After searching through case after case, Tammy spotted an impressive ring that was closer to the register and summoned the salesman over to inquire about it.

"I'd like to try that one on."

"Sure, just give me one second. These are our more expensive collection so I just need to get the key to unlock the case."

Jerome looked at Tammy but Tammy didn't even flinch. When she put it on, she spread her hand out. "This is nice. I could see myself wearing this. What do you think?" She turned her hand to Jerome but the only thing on his mind was what the salesman said before he went to get the key. He tried to play it cool though. "How much is this one?"

The salesman looked at the spot where the ring had been and without hesitation, "that would be fifty eight hundred."

"Dollars?" Jerome looked at Tammy wondering why she still had it on. Tammy seemed not to catch on to his look. "I like it."

Did she just hear the man? That's too expensive. Jerome addressed the salesman. "We're looking for something more in our price range."

"Sure. What would that be?" the salesman turned to Tammy in anticipation that she'd be handing him the ring back and she reluctantly did.

"Around a thousand," Jerome looked at Tammy.

Tammy was taken aback. She hadn't thought to ask Jerome about it earlier but she sure was now. She turned to the salesman, who had already started for the area that fell into the range Jerome had just spoken of. "Can you give us a minute?" Tammy didn't wait for a response, as she then turned back to Jerome.

"I didn't think to ask you about this earlier but what if I really want to get a more expensive ring? I really like that one."

"Tammy, we don't have the money for that. I think a thousand dollars is enough money for a decent ring," he tried to keep his voice to a whisper.

She mirrored his volume. "Yes, but all those rings look like something I've seen before. I want something unique."

Where is this coming from? Something unique? I don't have unique money. Jerome rubbed the back of his neck. "Tammy I can't afford a ring like that but I can afford a thousand dollar ring, I can even go up to fifteen hundred but I'm not going to tell *him* that."

"I understand but I'll pay the difference."

Jerome closed his eyes for a brief second, trying to stay calm. "No, you're not."

"Why?"

"What is it about this ring?"

"I'm not dead set on it. I still want to see some more places but I know I don't want something everybody else has so I know it'll be more expensive and I'm O.K. with it so I'll pay the difference of whatever you put down."

He shook his head adamantly. "That's not how this works. I'm not going to let you pay for your own wedding ring."

"But it's what I want. I'm the one who has to wear it. I don't see what the problem is."

"A man does not let his soon-to-be wife pay for her own ring. I won't do it. There are plenty of rings you can choose from. If you don't see something here, let's go somewhere else. And where is all this money coming from? You said you just got through paying off your student loans. We're not going into debt for any of this. If we can't afford it, we can't get it."

"I totally agree. I was just able to save up some money with all the overtime I'd been working and what better thing to spend it on than my ring that I'll be wearing for the rest of my life?"

"That's all fine. You can just spend it on something else like your dress or something but no, I won't let you spend your own money on your wedding ring."

Tammy sighed. "Well let's go to another store and maybe I'll see something there." Jerome obliged and told the salesman they may come back later and headed for the car but Tammy told him she had to use the bathroom and would be right there, that he could go ahead and cool the car off.

In the bathroom Tammy frantically dialed Laura's number and when she answered Tammy immediately asked to speak to Frank. She explained her dilemma to him and asked for his advice.

"Tammy, I agree with Jerome. No man wants to see you showing off your ring and know that you had to help him pay for it. No way."

"But I'm the one who has to wear it so I should be able to get what I want."

"Tammy, pick your battles, because you're not gonna win this one. You'll end up frustrating the man. You can always upgrade later on after you've been married for a few years, but for now just accept how much he says he can afford."

Silence.

"And Tammy, don't go behind his back and buy it either. I'm telling you now, you don't want to do that. That would really set him off. Just be patient."

There was another pause, this one longer than the last, as she thought about what he was saying and about the consequences her decision would have, not only for Jerome, but for their relationship. "Fine. O.K. I get it."

"Good. And drop the attitude. I hear it all in your voice."

Tammy gasped then relented, releasing a long stream of air. "Alright...and thank you."

"Anytime."

After hanging up, Tammy dropped her expectations and vowed not to make this anymore difficult for her fiancé. This is one sacrifice she'd have to swallow.

Chapter 34

Pronouncement

THE DAY HAD finally come. Tammy would stand in front of hundreds of people and profess her undying love to the man of her dreams, Jerome Davis. To her surprise, she woke up to the sound of rain drops hitting the roof that quickly turned into heavy rain, which was not in the forecast. Her mind raced. She was used to the unpredictability of Houston weather but today it had to behave. She said a quick prayer for the rain to stop and for the sky to be filled with nothing but sun. She wanted this day to be perfect.

The ladies slept over Jorge and Maria's house and the men over Frank and Laura's. You wouldn't really call it a bachelorette party, but a night of advice, reflection, and watching an old movie. The guys had pretty much taken Jerome under their wing and he was comfortable with them so he slept over there. Tammy was looking forward to sitting on the porch swing but looked through the bedroom window instead. She started reminiscing over the whirlwind of events in the last few years. She worked her tail off getting herself out of debt, then gets hooked up with some church members who started a church lottery pool, their whole lives change when they win ten million dollars, which she could have used to instantly pay off student loans and avoid all the late hours of overtime and fast food dollar menus, scrimping for every penny. And just when she thought she'd have no one to share it with, she meets Jerome. God sure has a sense of humor.

The smell of coffee brought her back to the present and she walked to the kitchen toward the voices of women already up.

"Good morning bride-to-be," Janet was the first to see her.

"Hi, Everyone."

"You ready for your big day?" Maria, the ultimate host, was still working in the kitchen finishing up what was sure to be another delicious meal. "You need to eat up because once you get to the reception, you'll be too busy to eat."

It was already midmorning and by the time they had eaten, cleaned up, and went over the final details of what Tammy wanted done at the church and the banquet hall, hours had flown by and it was time to get ready. Because she wanted to surprise Jerome and her parents, the rehearsal and dinner the night before were done in the fellowship hall not the sanctuary. It wasn't ideal for those in the wedding party but she had taken a picture of the sanctuary beforehand and had it at the ready whenever she needed to point out where people were to go. She thought it was quite clever, because she also didn't have to answer any of Jerome's inevitable questions of how much she really spent on everything. She'd give him an answer after the ceremony, not all the details of course but enough to satisfy him; the whole truth wouldn't come until years later.

After applying makeup and pinning her hair up in lose curls, Tammy made sure she had her heels, wedding dress, and jewelry. She placed the shoe bag over the hanger of the long bag that housed her gown and all of them headed for the limo already waiting outside.

"Oh, thank God." The sunlight beamed on her face as the front door opened. The weather had behaved and God had answered her prayer. The birds chirping in the trees above made her smile even more.

***

Jerome entered the sanctuary as the music played, the pews already filled to the brim with family and friends. He stopped in mid stride and almost tripped Larry who was walking closely behind him. "Is this my wedding?" He looked around the sanctuary like a child in a room full of gifts on Christmas morning. He was in awe of the sight.

White Ionic columns lined the entire pulpit as if they were in a Greek scene. Vertical grooves completely lined each column, only to be met at the bottom and top with intricate gold engravings. One extra embellishment the tops had that the bottoms did not, were two cylinders that connected like an open scroll, and lay perpendicular to the column, partially enclosing the top adornments like a covering. The entire sanctuary was dimmed and cascading lights hung from the air like stars in the sky. On the outside of each pew were small white trees with glassy light shining from every branch. The center aisle was roped off on both sides with what looked like clusters of stars engulfed in shear ribbons connecting each pew from front to back, each side bordering the personal lane his bride would soon walk down. The decorations were indeed breathtaking. It was a sea of white glass everywhere your eyes could see, like the attendees were all in a scene from a fairytale, while Jerome with his all white tuxedo on waited for his real-life princess to come walking down the aisle.

Another love song played as the ceremony continued. Both of their mothers were now seated, after lighting their respective candles on either side of the unity candle. An usher came to unroll a shimmery sheet that he pulled down the aisle, laying it on top of the white layer that was already there. The combination of which made the path look like a river of sparkling glass. The next song that bellowed from the speakers was The Wedding Song and as the double doors opened the house lights dimmed even more as a pair of soft lights shone on Jerome and Tammy, now in view just beyond the entry.

As everyone stood you could hear a few gasps and whispers as one person after another saw her. The gown shimmered as if containing hundreds of diamonds between each inch of lace. The scallop collar gave way to an elegant form fitting gown that touched the ground and opened up in the back to an oversized train. Her clear pumps on the glimmering walkway gave the illusion that she was barefoot. Tammy held her father's arm tighter as the two exchanged a glance and then began to walk down the aisle, the light illuminating her eyes and her smile.

Jerome was mesmerized by this one moment in time so much so that Larry had to nudge him because he had missed his cue to come take Tammy from her dad and walk her the few remaining steps to the front. She was so stunning, he couldn't take his eyes off of her. Her loose curls were sprinkled with light and her eye lashes protected the most alluring eyes. Her lips, topped only with a glossy finish, merely enhanced their natural color and begged to be caressed by his.

Tammy's heart pounded at the site of him. His double breasted suit could not hide his chiseled frame. She could feel the warmth of his body flow through her just with the touch of his hand. His eyes told her how much she meant to him. They both were full with so much emotion so Pastor had to make a joke to lighten the intensity. After Pastor David went through the protocol it was time for them to recite the vows they had written before they would say the traditional ones. Tammy went first.

"You came into my life when I least expected it. You interrupted my plans and gave me better ones. You filled a void I didn't know I had. And I can't imagine life without you. I know I've put you through some challenges but yet you still pursued me. Thank you for fighting for me. I can't wait to spend forever with you."

A few sniffles were scattered throughout the audience as the microphone was handed to Jerome. "I hope this day will be a reflection of our life together. This morning it was raining, and although I knew you would be disappointed, you kept getting ready, I kept getting ready and before you knew it, the sun was in the sky. Marriage is not easy and the trials of life will rain on us, storms may even come, but if we just keep doing what we are supposed to do, the sun will eventually shine. Always know the sun will shine again and together we can get through anything."

"Amen."

"Yes, it will."

The confirmations came from all areas of the sanctuary as Jerome continued, "Life before you came was just a blur. When I met you it seemed like everything before then didn't exist. When you told me how old you were and I figured out that you were seven years younger than me I thought about what I must have been doing when you were birthed into this world, because at that moment, God released my destiny. Seven years is the number of completion and my life wasn't complete until you were born. I feel like I've been waiting for you my whole life and now my life is just beginning."

Affirmations and applause filled the sanctuary and some even grabbed for tissue. The couple then exchanged wedding rings, Jerome with a platinum band and Tammy with a diamond-studded ring Jerome had custom made to complement her engagement ring which cleverly fit inside the wedding ring like a puzzle piece. After lighting the unity candle, Jerome and Tammy came back to the front for Pastor David to give the last words.

"You know marriage is a sacred vow. It's not something to be taken lightly; it's a covenant with God and your spouse. Many people today get married for the wrong reasons and divorce at the drop of a hat but marriage is supposed to be forever, till death do you part." Amen came from all directions. "I want you to remember that and not just you but everyone in here." He looked beyond Jerome and Tammy and into the mass of people watching intently. "And to help you remember…" Pastor reached into his pocket and pulled out two small sheer bags that were filled with a white substance. "These are bags of rice." He gave one to Jerome and Tammy. These bags represent you, all of you, all of your substance, your health, your experiences, your good things your bad things, everything that makes up you." He then reached inside his other pocket and pulled out a bigger bag and turned it upside down to show that it was empty. "Now pour your rice in here, both of you together." They did. "Now throw your bags on the floor." A trickle of laughter emerged from the audience. Pastor then pulled the strings, closing the bigger bag and handed it to Jerome. "Now, I want you to shake it." Jerome did. "Keep shaking it. Now give it to Tammy. Now you do the same thing." She obliged. "Alright now you two open up the bag," he paused for effect, "Now you try and get your own pieces of rice out of there. Tammy pick out yours, Jerome try to get yours out." The lesson was clear and Jerome tried to keep his composure while tears escaped from Tammy's eyes and rolled down her cheeks. She wasn't the only one. There were many teary-eyed supporters reaching for tissues and dotting their faces. "You are no longer separate individuals in the sight of God, you are now one. And what God has joined together, let no man put asunder. No separation, no divorce, you are one!"

"Say it."

"Yes."

"Hallelujah."

"Tell it."

The affirmations erupted from everywhere. The church was filled with cheers and applause and people were already standing all around the sanctuary. And with that Pastor David ended with, "I now pronounce you husband and wife."

Chapter 35

Ecstasy

DON TOUCHED JANET'S hand, softly caressing each finger. "Let's take it one day at a time," she said as she slowly pulled her hand away. Don blinked and shook his head in reluctant agreement.

"I just don't know if I can fall in love with you again. I don't know if I have the strength." Janet confessed.

Don hugged her, as a tear welled up in her eye, the first sign of raw emotion he'd seen that showed she *did* care. "I'll do whatever it takes," he assured her. "You've loved me when I wasn't always loveable and now that I know how to love, I'm not going to give the best of me to someone else. You've gone through everything else. Don't you want to see my best?" He sighed after Janet didn't respond. "I don't want to share my life with anyone but you. You will fall in love with me again. I'll be patient. Take all the time you need. I'm going to love you God's way from now on," Don insisted.

He caressed Janet's hair while she lingered in his embrace. Not knowing what else to say, Don continued to hold her in silence. After several minutes passed, Don asked, "Are you ready to join the others?"

Janet lifted her head from his chest and nodded. She closed her eyes in a failed attempt to stop the flow of tears, while Don gently wiped them away. Janet could tell that he had changed, but she had been afraid to believe the change was lasting. She didn't want to get her hopes up again. All she could really do was pray and ask God to restore her marriage and help her unbelief.

They started walking toward the designated meeting spot to join the others who had already arrived.

"What a view!" Maria exclaimed as Jorge pulled her in closer.

"Yes, this is breathtaking," Jorge gazed across the blue sea.

In close proximity stood Frank and Laura in a passionate embrace; their bodies sunken into each other in an uncharacteristic display of public affection. This marked a year and a half since their winning lottery numbers were pulled and the first real trip that any of them had taken due to the vow of normalcy everyone had agreed to. It was now time to really enjoy their winnings and the significance of the moment got the best of everyone.

Amanda was sitting on Craig's lap, both of them giggling back and forth like school kids, overjoyed with excitement.

As Don and Janet approached, walking hand in hand, everyone started to gather together.

After the long plane ride, they had all agreed to meet on the beach alongside the resort as soon as everyone had gotten their bags settled in their rooms.

"So, after all the madness, was it worth it?" Frank asked the group.

"After all we've been through, I wouldn't trade it for the world. This is living!" Craig said, Amanda nodding in agreement.

The conversation was cut short because the newly married Tammy and Jerome walked up, all smiles.

Everyone looked at each other as if to silently remind themselves not to say anything about the money, since Tammy still hadn't told Jerome yet. She informed Laura the day before that she couldn't wait any longer and was going to let him know on this trip. She was tired of concealing the costs of things and felt guilty keeping the secret from him. It was enough just to keep the true cost of the wedding from him. She didn't plan too much of an extravagant wedding considering she was a millionaire. And from what she'd heard other couples had spent on their wedding, she wasn't totally out of line, but it was clearly more than they would have been able to wisely afford on both of their salaries.

At the reception she was grateful to be able to send everyone home with a parting gift of a picture book that was made right there on the spot from a photography company she had hired. Out of all the hundreds of pictures that were taken before and during the wedding, and at the reception, everyone was able to look through the proofs and hand pick up to fifty pictures they wanted in their personal book. They were printed out before the end of the night and everyone left with a custom-made photo album of the wonderful occasion. And the ten-person band she hired was able to play everyone's favorites from any era.

Thank God no one else had any idea of what kind of money they made. People may have assumed Jerome and Tammy's parents helped pay for the wedding. Tammy even had to convince Jerome that she wasn't turning into a diva and spending too much money as a percentage of her income. She explained that she had saved up for a long time to have the wedding she'd envisioned as a child. His concerns were legitimate because he wanted to make sure they had a life after the expensive wedding was over and the amount of money he had budgeted for the wedding didn't compare to what he saw that afternoon.

So now had come the time for Tammy to come clean, and tell Jerome the truth of how she could afford to contribute so much money to their wedding. During Tammy's phone conversation with Laura, Frank had got on the line and told Tammy to make sure she told Jerome on the first night so they wouldn't have to monitor their speech around him, because someone was bound to slip up.

"Hey, Newlyweds!" and such were thrown at the couple as they approached.

"This place is amazing!" Tammy shrieked.

"I've never seen anything like this," Jerome agreed, shaking his head in awe and bewilderment as his eyes moved from the resort to the ocean.

As they joined the others, amidst the chatter, Jerome leaned over to Frank and quietly asked, "Man, how much did this set you back?" referring to the cost of the get-away trip.

Frank hesitated, looked Jerome straight in the eye and said, "Tammy has something to tell you."

Jerome rared back in his seat. There was no emotion on Frank's face so Jerome didn't know what that meant. Was Tammy an excessive spender hiding an addiction? How could that be when they went over their credit reports together? Did Tammy borrow the money for this trip from Frank and Laura? Jerome continued to look at Frank, asking him with his eyes, *Tell me what?* Franks only answer to that silent question was a head nod in Tammy's direction.

Jerome sat there for a moment, his mind still wondering. As every second lapsed, he thought of one explanation after another and with each passing thought, his imagination grew more negative; the elaborate wedding and reception, the mind-blowing dress, and this five-star resort. It wasn't his intention to think the worst, but that's all that kept popping up in his mind.

Jerome rubbed his palms together, clasped his hands a few times, then got up and walked over to Tammy. He whispered in her ear, and she cut her eyes at Frank. After a brief hesitation, she nodded in surrender.

"Will you excuse us?" she told rather than asked the group. The talking stopped and all eyes were on them. Tammy grabbed her husband's hand and as they walked off to a more private area, she turned her head and winked at her friends, signaling to them that the time had finally arrived to come clean.

Tammy's heart began to race. She had practiced this moment many times but now she was at a loss for words. How would she begin the conversation? What details should she include? Should she just come right out and say it? How will he react?

With the newlyweds gone, everyone still remained silent, as if any noise might threaten this pivotal moment. The only life audible were the outdoor sounds of nature. They waited, searching each other's thoughts with their eyes, not a word spoken, for what seemed liked ages. Then, in the distance,

"Whoooooooaaaaahhhh!!!!"

The magnitude of Jerome's loud scream pierced the stillness. It was a scream of excitement, of unbelief, of sheer happiness, and of possibilities. As if on cue, the rest of the group all laughed and toasted their champagne glasses. Now the real fun would begin.

TO BE CONTINUED...STAY TUNED FOR THE SEQUEL, The Win 2 - The Aftermath

You Can Help...

Thank you for reading this book. If you enjoyed it please take the time to **write a review**, even if it is one sentence; on Amazon.com or BN.com (Barnes and Noble), etc. Book reviews help other readers decide if they want to purchase this book, give valuable advice to me, the author, and ultimately increase book sales. **Will you help me reach my goal of 100 reviews on Amazon?** Thank you so much in advance!

Shalonda McFarland

An Offer For You

When you sign up for my notifications by entering your email address on the Contact Us portion of my website, ShalondaMcFarland.com, I will send you a FREE electronic version of one of my books. By signing up, you will also be one of the first to know about any of my FREE book promotions, new books, other specials, and exciting news. You can unsubscribe at any time.

Lottery List

What would you do or buy if you won a big lottery jackpot? List it here and compare your list with others for fun.

1. _____
2. _____
3. _____
4. _____
5. _____
6. _____
7. _____
8. _____
9. _____
10. _____
11. _____
12. _____
13. _____
14. _____
15. _____
16. _____
17. _____
18. _____
19. _____
20. _____

Lottery Stats

- Six states — Delaware, Kansas, Maryland, North Dakota, Ohio and South Carolina — allow lottery winners to remain anonymous.
  http://www.nbcnews.com/news/us-news/can-you-spare-million-why-it-pays-stay-anonymous-after-n70071
- 44% percent of lottery winners had spent their entire winnings within 5 years (Statistic Brain Research Institute)
- Biggest Lottery Win (Won on January 13, 2016), $1.5 Billion in Powerball, split between three winners from California, Tennessee, and Florida
- Most United States lottery wins are subject to 25% IRS tax withholdings
- 48% of winners keep their day job (TheRichest.com)
- 83% of winners give money to family (TheRichest.com)
- 90% of winners lose friends (TheRichest.com)
- The Texas Statutes under Gambling Laws, considers raffles and anything else where money is exchanged for a chance to win anything of value, a form of lottery, and therefore is gambling.
  http://www.gambling-law-us.com/State-Laws/Texas/

Bibliography

David Haugen and Susan Musser, book editors. *Gambling.* Farmington Hills, MI: Greenhaven Press, 2007.

Nibert, David Alan. *Hitting the lottery jackpot: state governments and the taxing of dreams.* New York, NY: Monthly Review Press, 2000.

Naspl.org

StatisticBrain.com

TheRichest.com

Pagliarini, Robert. "5 Rules if you play an office lottery pool." *Forbes.com* p., 11 Dec. 2013 Web. 10 Aug. 2016

Powerball.com

LaFleurs.com

Naspl.org (North American Association of State and Provincial Lotteries)

ncpgambling.org

Zell, Wayne M. "Using LLC or Trust to Receive Lottery Winnings" *The National Law Review,* Web. 12 Jan. 2016

Song of Solomon 4 New American Standard Bible NASB)

McFarland, Mariah. "Baby Gurl," 2017.

https://www.texasattorneygeneral.gov/cpd/the-3-day-right-to-cancel-a-purchase

Book Discussion

From Chapter 1

1. Is it permissible for Christians to play the lottery or go to the casino?
2. Even if you feel it *is* permissible, should Christians partake in such activity?
3. What does the Bible say about gambling?
4. Discuss the differences and similarities between gambling, the lottery, the stock market and a church raffle.

From Chapter 2

5. If you have been in a lottery pool, share your experience.
6. If you wanted to start a lottery pool, who would you include and why?
7. Would your lottery pool include a certain group, such as your friends, family, or organization, i.e. your church or job?
8. What rules would you want to make sure are adhered to?

From Chapter 3

9. Discuss child support and visitation dynamics.
10. If you are or have been in this scenario, what has worked and not worked?

11. What suggestions do you have for both the custodial and non-custodial parent?

12. Sometimes the parent who gets child support uses the child as a pawn to get back at the other parent, not realizing it hurts the child. Discuss this.

From Chapter 4

13. How would you react to Craig and Amanda not paying their share that month? Should they be included in the winnings? Why or why not?

14. Does your answer change if you are Craig and Amanda?

From Chapter 6

15. It took Tammy four years to pay off her student loans, is it possible to get a degree without taking out loans? (It is possible so discuss how.)

16. Discuss how a man is to find a wife, and not the other way around.

From Chapter 7

17. Discuss Janet's statement, "Money doesn't change you, it just magnifies who we are." Do you agree or disagree?

18. How should Pastor David respond to the donation?

19. If he should accept the offering, what should Pastor David do with the money? And is your answer ministry or activity based? (Considerations may include blessing certain members, foreign missions, take a percentage as a love offering, buy cars and raffle them off at a church function, etc.)

20. If he should not accept, why?

21. Gambling has been called a tax on the poor. Given the fact that gambling is voluntary, what are your thoughts about the before statement?

22. Given our nation's history of using lotteries to fund war efforts, reconstruction, and now education (although some say too small of a percentage goes to education), what would you propose lottery revenues go toward?

23. Should Internet gambling be banned to protect children?

From Chapter 8

24. What are your thoughts about Laura paying off her parents' home and back taxes?

25. If you were to pay off someone's home and then they turned around and got an equity line of credit against the home or a reverse mortgage, how would you feel?

26. Would that be a good use of God's resources?

27. Regarding Frank's situation with his mother, what do the scripture verses below mean when they say to honor your parents? What does that look like?

*Honour thy father and mother; which is the first commandment with promise…**Ephesians 6:2 KJV***

Honour thy father and thy mother: that thy days may be long upon the land which the LORD thy God giveth thee. ***Exodus 20:12 KJV***

28. What does the scripture *not* mean?

29. Who are considered your parents? Are step-parents, legal guardians, or adoptive parents included?

30. Do you draw the line and if so where do you draw the line between honoring parents who've lied, manipulated, mistreated, or abused you?

From Chapter 10

31. Whose responsibility is it to pay for college, or any higher education; the son/daughter or the parent? Why?

32. When a parent pays child support, should they also help with college?

33. As far as parents using kids as pawns, have you been the perpetrator or the victim in this situation? If so, please discuss your insight.

34. How does one maintain a relationship with their child, when the other parent is unwilling to cooperate?

35. Should a mother be given custody of a son or can only a man raise a boy effectively?

From Chapter 11

36. What are your thoughts about a prenup? Would you be offended if your soon-to-be spouse asked you to sign one? If you have a lot of money does your answer change?

37. Should you tithe off of winnings from gambling, whether from the lottery, casino, bingo, etc?

38. Should your tithes go to the church or to a cause/organization you deem worthy?

39. Should your tithes just go to the church you attend or can it be split up and go to other churches?

40. Is it possible to be a member of more than one church, at the same time?

From Chapter 14

41. What are your thoughts about asking the person you are in a serious relationship with to see their credit report?

42. What about your spouse?

43. If they refuse, is that a concern?

**You can get a free yearly credit report from the three credit bureaus at AnnualCreditReport.com

To get a free report every four months, don't request all three reports at the same time. Space out your requests to a different credit bureau every four months and rotate the requests. Ex) Get one from Equifax in January, Experian in April, and TransUnion in August, then repeat the cycle each year.

From Chapter 15

44. How should a church determine who to help and who not to help?

45. Should a church only help their own members, who usually have contributed to the ministry in some way, or limit it just to their tithing members?

46. Should a church help anyone who comes off the street asking for assistance? What procedures should be put in place to protect the church from people who would abuse that assistance?

47. If you, as a tithing church member fall on hard times, do you expect your church to help you? Why? How?

48. How does the church hold people accountable for changing their bad habits, bad choices, etc. regarding finances?

49. How many times should the church give money to someone who requests help?

50. Is it ever acceptable for the church to give money to someone, or should the church direct them to any variety of social services?

51. What amount is acceptable for the church to give to help someone and also break the cycle of bad financial habits?

52. Should the church be the first resort, last resort, or no resort in terms of someone asking the church for assistance?

53. What financial teaching should the church provide to help others live financially-responsible lives?

From Chapter 18

54. When is it appropriate to tell your fiancé/spouse that you've won a windfall or significant inheritance?

55. What are your thoughts on giving someone money or a vehicle for example, without teaching them how to manage it?

From Chapter 19

56. Maury commented that church folk don't play the lottery because God will make a way. Is playing the lottery showing a lack of faith in God?

57. Is there such a thing as going to church too often, as Maury joked?

From Chapter 22

58. If you were the pastor, how would you handle the money?

59. Discuss all the pastors' perspectives on gambling. Which ones do you agree with? How does that compare to what the Bible says?

60. Is there anything wrong with having a church-sponsored lottery, normally called a raffle? (selling or asking for donations in exchange for a chance to win something; e.g. a trip, T.V., gift basket, etc.)

61. How would you feel if your church sponsored a gambling trip to a casino, bingo hall, or started a lottery pool?

From Chapter 31

62. What percentage of a couple's income should be spent on a wedding?

63. Discuss any legitimate reasons why a couple would spend "too much" money on a wedding and could this be the first test of how to handle financial issues in their marriage?

Lottery Pool Tips

1. Immediately sign the back of the ticket(s).
2. Put everything in writing. If it's not in writing, it never happened.
3. Write down the rules and have every member sign it. Also make them initial beside any lines of particular importance.
4. Include provisions of what happens if someone doesn't pay.
5. Make the rule that no one can buy a personal lottery ticket for the particular game that the lottery pool is participating in.
6. Either make copies (or take a picture and send via text message to everyone) of the tickets immediately after buying them.
7. If you win big, establish a blind trust or LLC to keep everyone's names out of the public.
8. There are a vast amount of suggestions on the internet. Just search "lottery pool."

Frequently Asked Questions

1. Did you win the lottery? **Answer:** No! (I can't help but smile each time I'm asked this question.) I don't really even play unless the pot is so high that it's talked about on the news, then I'll go get me one or two tickets.
2. Do you pick your numbers or let the system pick? **Answer:** I let the system pick. It's more efficient for me.
3. Do you gamble at casinos, etc? **Answer:** I have in the past and have not ruled out ever doing it again. I only play twenty to thirty dollars max, the whole trip. Once the money is gone, that's it.

About the Author

SHALONDA MCFARLAND is an author, speaker, and Gospel recording artist. She has dedicated her life to the glory of God specializing in youth ministries where she has been teaching, speaking, and volunteering for over twenty years. Worst Witness Ministry, which Shalonda birthed out of her book and workbook *A Christian's Worst Witness...From Being Broke To Being Blessed* is focused on teaching Christians how to handle money God's way. Her articles on Christian finance have been featured in various church mediums and Christian publications, including magazines and journals.

Mrs. McFarland is a dynamic, heart-felt, action-provoking speaker, who delivers a biblically-based message diverse with everyday examples and strives to live out her personal brand of *serving by adding value and exceeding expectations.*

Shalonda and her husband Doug have five children, Rakaya, Doug Jr., Mariah, Jordan, and Melanie, and reside in the Houston, Texas area.

Made in the USA
Lexington, KY
01 July 2018